# PRAISE FOR EFRÉN DIVIDED

"The beautiful and gripping novel sheds light on the horrific consequences of separating families. It will reshape discussions about immigration and change hearts for the better. This debut announces an important new writer on the scene."

—Fred Aceves, author of *The Closest I've Come* and *The New David Espinoza*

"A stunning, masterful, and timely debut. Cisneros balances both the despair of a family torn apart by US immigration policies and the loving determination of a boy to bridge the divide."

—David Bowles, author of *They Call Me Güero* and coauthor of *The Chupacabras of the Río Grande*

"A moving portrayal of the shame, fear, and uncertainty of a family ripped apart."

—Aimée Medina Carr, author of *River of Love*

"Cisneros handles the timely subject matter with heart, depth, and authenticity, leaving readers like me hopeful and determined to make this world a better place for all children."

—Angela Cervantes, author of *Gaby, Lost and Found* and *Lety Out Loud*

"Ernesto Cisneros has captured the richness, beauty, and love of working-class Mexican immigrant families in his much-needed debut. *Efrén Divided* can be counted among those books that will inspire young people to action, activism, and change in their communities."

—e.E. Charlton-Trujillo, author of *Fat Angie*

"This book is a call to not take the world as it is, but to fight for the world as it should be."

—Adrianna Cuevas, author of *The Total Eclipse of Nestor Lopez*

# EFRÉN

# DIVIDED

## A NOVEL BY
## ERNESTO CISNEROS

Quill Tree Books
An Imprint of HarperCollinsPublishers

Quill Tree Books is an imprint of HarperCollins Publishers.

Efrén Divided
Copyright © 2020 by Ernesto Cisneros

Library of Congress Cataloging-in-Publication Data
Names: Cisneros, Ernesto, author.
Title: Efrén divided : a novel / by Ernesto Cisneros.
Description: First edition. | New York, NY : Harper, 2020. | Audience:
     Ages 3–7 | Audience: Grades 4–6 | Summary: While his father works
     two jobs, seventh-grader Efrén Nava must take care of his twin
     siblings, kindergartners Max and Mía, after their mother is deported
     to Mexico. Includes glossary of Spanish words
Identifiers: LCCN 2019027332 | ISBN 9780062881687 (hardcover) | ISBN
     9780062881694 (paperback)
Subjects: CYAC: Deportation—Fiction. | Illegal aliens—Fiction. |
     Schools—Fiction. | Brothers and sisters—Fiction. | Twins—Fiction. |
     Mexican Americans—Fiction.
Classification: LCC PZ7.1.C568 Efr 2020 | DDC [Fic]—dc23
     LC record available at https://lccn.loc.gov/2019027332

Typography by David DeWitt
22 23 24 25  PC/BRR  12 11 10
❖
First paperback edition, 2021

*For my children, for leading me to write this book.*
*We dedicate it to all immigrant families who continue*
*to be cruelly separated and, especially, to all the brave*
*children who are forced to live this story.*

*Now the Star-bellied Sneetches*
*had bellies with stars.*
*The Plain-bellied Sneetches*
*had none upon thars.*

*The stars weren't so big;*
*they were really quite small.*
*You would think such a thing wouldn't matter at all.*

—DR. SEUSS

# ONE

Once again, Efrén Nava woke up to a chubby pajamaed foot in his face. He squinted at the bright yellow rays peeking in through the broken window blinds and looked to his left. But it wasn't Mía's foot. She was fast asleep, cuddled at the edge of their mattress with the same naked plush doll whose clothes she'd taken off and lost a long time ago.

He looked to his right . . . sure enough, the foot belonged to Max. How Max managed to roll over Efrén during the middle of the night was beyond him. Efrén shook his head and sighed. But then he caught sight of a tiny hole on the right foot of his little brother's flannel onesie. Smiling, Efrén licked the tip of his pinky and gave a wet willy to Max's pudgy toe.

Efrén covered his mouth and stifled his laughter as a sleeping Max pulled away his leg. However, the victory didn't last long. Max spun around in his sleep and planted his other foot in Efrén's face.

There was no way to win. Efrén yawned himself fully awake before turning toward his parents' side of the room. Once again, Apá was gone. No sign of his heavy jacket or scuffed-up work boots by the front door either. It seemed no matter how early Efrén tried getting up, he just couldn't catch Apá getting ready for work.

Amá was the same way and never slept in. Any minute now, she'd wake up, unwrap her blankets, and go right to the kitchen to make breakfast. There was a potful of leftover frijoles from last night's dinner, and that meant she would for sure be making fresh sopes this morning—Efrén's favorite.

But before that, Efrén had something important to do. He lifted Max's leg by the pajamas and got up, careful not to disturb Mía, who now snuggled close to Max.

Efrén stepped over the pair of pint-sized legs and arms blocking his path. He wasn't sure which was worse, sharing a mattress with two kindergartners or sharing the bathroom. Their apartment was really one big room, so the only place he could find peace and quiet was the bathroom.

Efrén looked in the mirror, wincing as he removed the tiny strips of tape pinning his ears back against the sides of his head—an idea he came up with after repeatedly hearing Amá warn the little ones against making funny faces.

"Sus caras se les van a quedar así," she'd say.

*Their faces freezing . . .* That's exactly what Efrén counted on.

It was only a theory . . . but if it were even slightly true, he guessed the same would apply to his ears. If he could manage to tape back his ears often enough, they too would eventually freeze and finally stop sticking out. All he had to do was make sure they folded in just the right way for a few more weeks and presto! Normal ears that didn't stick out like the knobs on Frankenstein's neck.

After taking care of business, Efrén climbed inside the empty bathtub with a library copy of *There's a Boy in the Girls' Bathroom,* by one of his favorite authors, Louis Sachar. Efrén loved reading books—even when he'd read them before. It was like visiting an old friend.

The main character, Bradley Chalkers, was the best. And it wasn't just that he had a really sweet side to him that his classmates didn't get to see. Nope. The boy was super tough and no matter how rough things got for him, he continued to show up and fight. Like Efrén's best friend, David. Another misunderstood kid.

Some kids at school only saw this white kid who likes to dress flashy and flaunt his latest piece of jewelry. But Efrén knew the real David. The same boy who once took off the sweatshirt he was wearing and donated it for a clothing drive in the neighborhood.

Normally, Efrén would lie in the tub reading and laughing until a stampede of feet came running toward the door. But this morning, his eyelids were extra heavy and the need for sleep was too powerful. He couldn't fight it, not after staying up so late waiting for Amá to return from working overtime hours at the factory.

For the last couple of weeks, there'd been a whole lot of talk, a whole lot of chisme (especially around the laundromat) about various raids and stop points happening around town. Efrén tried not thinking about what he'd seen on the news, all the stories about families being separated, kids put in cages. But that was easier said than done.

Efrén couldn't help but worry. Despite numerous lectures from Amá—and repeated threats of being on the receiving end of her chancla—he stayed up really late until she got home.

He'd done the best he could to piece together the information he heard, but it wasn't easy. It seemed like anytime he caught adults talking about it, someone in the room would nod toward him and the topic would shift to something else—usually the final minutes of the previous night's telenovela.

After an unplanned nap in the tub, Efrén heard rattling in the kitchen and headed over. By the stove stood Amá, wearing her fuzzy blue robe that according to Max made her look like the Cookie Monster. Efrén stood and admired how easily Amá formed perfect little saucers from the doughy masa de maíz and then pinched the steaming edges to form a tiny wall to keep the beans from seeping off.

Her hands were tough and hummingbird-fast as she tested the griddle's temperature by touching it with her bare fingers. *How did she manage not to burn herself?* Efrén wondered.

Amá's sopes were delicious. And even though they weren't much more than a thick corn tortilla topped with beans and fresh Ranchero cheese, Efrén didn't think of them as a poor person's meal. To him . . . to Max . . . to Mía, they were a special treat. Just one of the many milagros Amá performed on a daily basis—something super.

*Super sopes . . . Sopers!*

That made Amá Soperwoman. Efrén laughed to himself. The word fit her perfectly.

Before long, Max and Mía were up and climbed onto their usual seats at the table. "¡Sopes!" They turned to each other and sprang out into song: "Frijoles, frijoles, de las comidas más ricas, ¡lo más que comes, lo más que pitas!"

Efrén shook his head. "You guys should be practicing your English. My fifth-grade teacher, Mrs. O'Neal, used to say that's the only way to master the language."

"Aquí están." Amá set the breakfast spread on the kitchen table, her exhausted eyes creasing as she smiled. "Mijo, most of the world speaks more than one language. And Spanish is a part of who we are." She moved toward Efrén and ruffled his hair. "You'll understand when you're older."

Max and Mía reached in first, each picking up a bean-and-cheese-topped sope.

Efrén eyed the last one while Amá filled the glasses with chilled orange juice.

"Amá, where is yours?"

"Ay, amor . . . a cup of cafecito is all I need."

Efrén's stomach grumbled, but it was his heart giving the orders. "Amá, why don't you take mine? I can have breakfast at school anyway. There's no point letting all that school food go to waste."

"And have them think I can't provide for my own children? No, gracias."

Efrén inhaled. "Ay, Amá," he said, knowing that she was simply being, well . . . Amá.

She pulled out a nopal she'd cut yesterday from the cactus plant peeking over the neighboring fence and matter-of-factly scraped off the thorns with a knife. Then she held it over the stovetop bare-handed. When it was well roasted, she scooped up the remainder of the beans with a wooden spoon and created a sort of cactus taco. "See? I'm fine," she said, taking a bite.

Being Soperwoman wasn't just about checking teeth, flattening down cowlicks, and making sure Max wore only one pair of underwear at a time. It included making sure that everyone wore perfectly creased pants and that any holes made the day before were creatively sewn or patched over.

"It's one thing to not have a lot of money," Amá reminded them just about every morning, "it's another to look the part."

Of all the things Amá did, this baffled Efrén the most. How could a person who sometimes spent seventy-plus hours a week locked in a factory behind a steaming iron go anywhere near one at home? Then again, this probably explained her talent for bare-handedly flipping tortillas and carrying them to the kitchen table without even a wince.

"Okay, mijos. Time to get ready for school."

Everyone knew the drill. Put on the clothes neatly laid out last night by Amá, brush teeth, comb hair, and then grab backpack with lunch inside.

Amá was about to hand out "well-done" kisses when out of nowhere, a helicopter hovered and roared uncomfortably close overhead. Amá waved a fist. "Ay, this is the second time in three weeks!" Unfortunately, sometimes the nighttime activities from the neighborhood carried over into the daytime hours. Home raids, car chases, and suspects at large were all as familiar as paletero trucks selling ice-cream bars outside of church.

Amá marched to the front door and locked the metal screen. Going into lockdown mode, Max and Mía shut and locked the sliding glass door in the back of the apartment before Amá could even ask.

No one spoke a word, listening for screaming, sirens, or worse . . . gunfire.

Amá peeked through the layered curtains she'd sewn together last year. "It was just passing by."

Amá had barely unlocked the door before the twins rushed past her and ran outside.

"Niños, don't run down the . . . stairs." She turned to Efrén, who was busy strapping on his backpack. "What am I going to do with those two?"

"Adoption?"

Amá playfully slapped the back of his head before stepping outside.

The twins waited by Don Ricardo's food truck parked curbside. "Can we get some chet-tos?"

Efrén rolled his eyes. "Guys, for the last time, they're called CHEETOS."

Amá smiled and waved off Don Ricardo (or Don Tapatío, as most of the neighborhood called him because of the huge mustache and sombrero that he wore). "No, gracias," she said. "Tal vez después de la escuela."

Don Ricardo returned the smile and nodded as she steered the twins away by their arms.

". . . if you are good," she added.

Amá and Efrén followed the twins into the kindergarten playground. Even though the school was only a sprint away, Amá never let them go alone—not even Efrén, whose middle school was only blocks away.

Between the swings and patch of dirt used for playing marbles, Max and Mía bear-hugged their favorite teacher, Ms. Solomon. She was an older lady, dressed in a gray business suit and clashing white sneakers. Eventually, they let her go and ran off to play on the jungle gym.

Amá approached the teacher for a hug herself.

"Señora Nava," Ms. Solomon asked. "¿cómo está?"

"Excelente, Maestra. Excelente."

Ms. Solomon turned to Efrén. "And you, Señorito, are getting almost too big to hug—almost." She leaned in and hugged him too.

Even with the air inside him being squeezed out, Efrén continued to smile.

Ms. Solomon paused to examine him once more. "I can't believe how big you're getting. Reminds me of how old I'm getting."

"You're not old, Ms. Solomon," Efrén answered. "You look exactly the same as when you taught me."

And of course, that made her laugh.

"Buenos días," Amá chimed in. "How have my little ones been behaving?"

Ms. Solomon turned and scrunched her lips to one side. "Just one tiny problema," she said, following with a short chuckle. "Yesterday, Max decided to hide underneath the sink and Mía would not stop crying until we found him."

That was typical Max. Unlike Mía, Max was born with his umbilical cord wrapped around his neck. Sadly, all the minutes Max went without oxygen hurt his brain. Made it hard for him to learn. Something he would have to deal with all of his life. Amá said it was a milagro that he survived at all. Efrén couldn't help but wonder what Max would've been like had the doctors caught the problem in time.

"Yeah, it's amazing how much Mía worries about him."

"I think it's super sweet." Suddenly, Ms. Solomon's face lit up. "Oh, before I forget. I already submitted your name for this year's Christmas gift baskets. I know it's still November, but I wanted to make sure that you were included. Especially after all the help you gave me putting together the costumes for last month's play."

"Gracias, Maestra," said Amá, "but we already got our turn. It's best if somebody else gets it this year."

Ms. Solomon pressed her lips together. "Oh, all right," she said. "But I do have a favor to ask."

"Ms. Solomon, after everything that you have done for my children, no favor is too big. Consider it done."

"Well,"—she leaned in closer to Amá—"I have a date. He's really cute," she said, giddy with excitement.

Efrén made a face and turned toward the playground.

"And he's a doctor!" she added. "I promised to cook dinner for him and was hoping to get the recipe for that fabulous mole you make."

Amá turned to Efrén. "Efrén, mijo. You've been asking me for weeks now. How would you feel about walking to school by yourself?"

"¿Solo?" he asked.

"Solito," she added.

Efrén fist pumped the air and shuffled his feet in a celebratory dance. "Can I go home and pick up my bike?"

"Only if you take your helmet."

He scowled at the thought of showing up to school

wearing the turtle-shaped helmet Amá bought him from the swap meet.

"No, thanks. I'll walk instead."

With that, Efrén darted past the portable classroom by the kindergarten side of campus and onto Highland Street. He passed Doña Chana's lime-colored duplex and paused to look at her guayaba tree where he scanned the branches.

Guayabas were his favorite, but that wasn't the kind of fruit he could picture any of his teachers eating. He figured teachers wouldn't accept anything coming from grubby-kid hands unless it came with a thick peel. Guayabas were definitely out. That was the thing about Highland Street: some people just saw the worn apartments and graffiti-tagged walls, but it offered good things too—like the fruit trees as far as the eye could see. According to Amá, it had to do with people her age being used to growing their own food.

That was one of the beautiful things about walking this street—even though people on the block didn't have much, everyone still shared and looked out for each other.

Efrén strolled a bit further, stopping at the apartment complex sandwiched in the middle of the block.

Up high in an avocado tree, a litter of black kittens competed for his attention.

"Hey, kitties. You guys might be cute, but I'm allergic to you."

Only the kittens didn't pay any mind to what he said and continued looking down at him and purring in their kitty language.

"No . . . it's not going to work. I have to get going or I'm going to be late for school. So stop it, I don't care how cute you guys are."

A few minutes later, Efrén found himself with red, itchy eyes, sitting up in the branches with two kitties nestled on his lap.

That's when a familiar whistle caught his attention.

Efrén looked down. Sure enough, it was David on his bike. Even though he was the only white kid living on this block, it wasn't his skin color that made him stand out—it was his hip-hop style. Kids on the block called him el Periquito Blanco because of the bright colors and baggy, oversized clothes he wore. That and his parrot-like nose. It'd been this way since he moved into the neighborhood.

Efrén carefully handed off the kittens to David and climbed on down.

"Whatcha doing up there?" asked David, kneading the kittens' backs.

"I was going to take some avocados to my teachers, but they're still kind of hard. They look like grenades."

"You ever held a real grenade?"

Efrén scratched the tip of his nose. "Not a real one. You?"

"Nope"—David pointed to his ears—"How about real diamonds, though?"

Efrén leaned in for a better look. "Man," he exclaimed. "Sweet earrings."

David smiled, showing off his new fake diamond-stud earrings large enough to cover his entire earlobes.

"Yeah . . . and they're real too."

Efrén leaned in even closer. "Real fake, you mean."

David crumpled his forehead. "No way. Not these. Don Tapatío wouldn't have charged me ten bucks if they were fake." He pointed at his ear. "Puro bling-bling," he said with a grin.

"Well, they're way cool."

"I know, right?" David surveyed the street. "Dude, where's your mom?"

Efrén shrugged. "Oh, I finally complained. Told her that I'm too old to be walked to school."

David scoffed. "Yeah, right. You probably begged her, huh?"

"Yeah, pretty much."

"Hey, wanna ride?"

"Sure." Efrén jumped onto the handlebars and held on tight. Initially, the bike swayed back and forth, but it eventually straightened as David made it onto the side of the street.

"You sure you can handle my weight?" Efrén asked.

"Of course. I gave Concha a ride the other day. And she's not all bony like you."

Efrén laughed.

"Yep . . ." David continued, "she barely squeezed between the handlebars."

Amá would have had a cow if she'd known they'd been riding together like that. As much as she liked David, she didn't quite understand him. Said she couldn't get why a boy would dye his hair different colors each month, or why he insisted on sagging his pants so low that she always knew the exact pattern of his boxer shorts.

Once, she even threatened to throw away all of Efrén's underwear if he ever tried something like that. And even though she was smiling when she said it,

Efrén knew better than to risk it.

Today though, Efrén felt like a real-life celebrity strutting his stuff down the red carpet. He sat upright waving at all the elementary school kids still being escorted by *their* overly protective mothers. *That's right, world. Eat your heart out!*

For once, he knew what it was like to be independent . . . like David. In all the time Efrén had known David, he'd never seen anyone calling him inside when it got late. Never saw anyone come out to the playground to see if he needed a sweater or hassle him for not keeping his shirt tucked all the way into his pants.

When the duo reached the school, David stopped at the bike rack where the school security guard, Rabbit, was standing. At least that's what kids called him. They thought it was a clever name for the old man who was so slow that a tortoise could outrace him.

Efrén hopped off the bike and untucked his shirt. "So what's up with you? You usually get here right before the late bell."

"Simple. You are looking at this year's new ASB President."

"A-S-B?"

"Associate something. I don't know. Point is, I'm

gonna run for school president. I know. I'm only a seventh-grader, but so is Jennifer Huerta, and she's the only other person running. She's such a teacher's pet. There's no way I'm gonna lose to her."

"You do know that's a bunch of extra work, right?"

"I know. But the way I figure, once I win, I can pass a new rule for the vice president to have to do all that stuff."

Efrén crinkled his forehead. "Dude, I don't think that's how it works."

"Of course not. That's why I'm running. To fix it. You know what . . . you should run for office too!"

"But then I'd have to do all your work."

"Or . . . you could be treasurer." He slid his fingers over his palm as if peeling a potato. "It's gonna rain money for sure. And you'll be in charge of it all. Dude, we're talking millions!"

Efrén shook his head. "I don't know about that. Besides, I'm not really into politics."

"Forget politics. I'm talking instant popularity. By next year, we'll both have our pick of girls."

"So *that's* what this is about?"

David went all puppy-eyed, a look Efrén had seen plenty of times before.

"Nah. No, thanks."

"Fine," said David. "But will you at least go with me to the candidates' meeting?"

Efrén knew all too well how horribly wrong most of David's plans usually went. Still, he couldn't say no to his best friend. "All right, but you owe me."

"Duh, dude! That's how politics works."

# TWO

When Rabbit arrived to open the gate, the boys locked up David's bike and headed inside to the principal's conference room. Across the main entrance stood a huge yellow banner. ASB SCHOOL ELECTIONS ARE COMING! The message was written in rounded letters with the O's in the shape of balloons. No doubt Ms. Salas's handiwork. She loved to decorate her letters every chance she got. And since she ran the ASB Leadership class, she had plenty of practice making school posters.

Efrén pulled on the door and propped it open with his foot. "After you, Mr. President."

David hiked up his pants. "I could *so* get used to this."

"Yeah, I bet." Efrén could see Ms. Salas along

with Jennifer Huerta and her super quiet sidekick, Han Pham, waiting inside. "Should I announce your arrival?"

"Nah, I got this," David said, his usual swag now replaced with an uncomfortable wobble from the wedgie he'd inadvertently given himself.

"Bienvenidos, niños," said Ms. Salas, standing over a pink box filled with different colored conchas. The tire-like thread of brown, yellow, and pink sugar coating made the bread look like the 4x4 tires off a toy Tonka truck. "Thank you for your interest in public service. What positions are you here for?"

David tapped his chest. "Just me . . . for school president."

She turned to Efrén. "Are you sure? We do have a few positions open if you're interested."

Efrén shook his head. "No, thank you. I'm just here to support David."

Ms. Salas pressed her lips together. "Back when I was a kid, school elections were a big deal. One year, we had eleven candidates. But that was then. Well, anyway . . . would you two boys like a concha? They're freshly baked."

Efrén remembered what Amá had taught him about

minding his manners, about accepting things from other people. "Don't be a 'pediche,'" she'd say.

She had this theory about how people only offer things because they feel obligated by the whole manners thing—kind of like when the family has company and Amá offers to feed them despite the fact that it would mean digging into the family's weekly rations.

So Efrén shook his head, hoping for a second request before accepting a piece.

But not David. No way. He had already snatched up a yellow and a brown concha before Ms. Salas had even offered any. "That's fine boys. We've got plenty for seconds . . ." She sighed, looking at the empty chairs around the conference table. "And thirds. And fourths. Possibly fifths."

The turnout *was* low, and since only the students who attended the meeting could run for office, it meant these two girls, Jennifer and Han, were all that stood in the way of David's presidency.

For the most part, Jennifer was a nice girl, but she had a habit of always raising her hand in class, whether the teacher asked a question or not. Not to mention automatically correcting anyone who messed up an answer—including teachers.

But Efrén didn't mind her. He thought she usually made good points.

As for Han, she didn't say much. In fact, kids at school simply referred to her as "that girl who sits next to Jennifer."

During the short meeting, Ms. Salas went into great detail about each of the ASB job descriptions and expectations.

Ms. Salas explained how with only two candidates running, the loser would automatically be given the vice president position.

Efrén studied David's competition, especially the way the girls locked onto Ms. Salas's every word and took careful notes.

And David? Well, he just slouched back, paying attention only to the sugary bread sitting across from him. Not exactly presidential behavior.

Still, Jennifer had a way of rubbing students the wrong way. A lot of kids didn't like that she seemed to know everything (a possible side effect of the fact that she always seemed to be reading).

David definitely stood a good chance. His cool swag and carefree attitude could go a long way against her. He might actually win.

Efrén and David raced to their first class after the ASB meeting ended. Mr. Garrett was not someone to mess with. Rumor had it that he was the only teacher at school to ever send an entire classroom to the principal's office. All at one time!

The strange thing about Mr. Garrett was that he wasn't always like this. Last year, during the sixth-grade Renaissance assembly, the principal, Mrs. Carey, introduced him as the district's teacher of the year.

Mr. Garrett ran up to the stage, high-fiving kids on his way. Everyone in the gymnasium stood and cheered. Mr. Garrett was all smiles that day and seemed like a totally different person. Since Mr. Garrett taught only honors history, Efrén knew he'd be having him the following year. Efrén couldn't wait.

Only something happened to him. It was as if a gray cloud swept down and planted itself right over Mr. Garrett's classroom and never left. He just didn't look happy anymore.

Efrén entered the classroom first. Unlike others around the school, this room stood bare, without any cheesy history teacher posters or bright bulletin boards highlighting student learning. Not here. Nada. Even Mr. Garrett's desk was bare—just the usual oversized mug of Starbucks coffee.

Not waiting for the bell, Efrén began copying down the homework. *ARTICLE OF THE DAY*, same as yesterday.

Everyone opened their assigned Chromebooks and began logging in. Mr. Garrett took his usual seat behind his desk. "You all know the drill. Work on the typing tutorial if you finish early." With that, he went back to the same book of sudoku puzzles from a week ago.

Just as Efrén positioned his fingers across the keyboard, a crumpled sheet of paper struck the back of his head. There was no need to look around or track the path it came from. This was just the way David preferred to communicate during class.

Efrén spread the paper across the desk, ironing it out as best he could. This particular note was an illustration—or "masterpizza," as David liked to call them.

The artwork on the page showed Mr. Garrett slumped over his desk with his face soaking in a pool of drool. A stick figure girl stood behind him with her finger resting inside her triangle nose. The speech bubble above her said, "You forgot to assign us homework!" It could be only one girl—Jennifer Huerta, David's new political enemy.

Efrén pressed down on his temples and buried the drawing under his Chromebook. He then turned back and shook his head at wide-grinning David.

As much he loved hanging around with David, Efrén chose to spend his morning nutrition breaks at his favorite place at school, the library. Like his bathtub at home, it was a place where he could open a book and let himself be taken anywhere he wanted.

Here, Efrén felt free.

Here, there was never anyone he needed to bathe or help with homework.

Here, he didn't have to take on security watch and sit by his apartment window at night, waiting for Amá to make it home safely from work.

Here, it was all about his escaping into other worlds where everything usually ended in smiles.

Efrén unzipped his backpack and took out the books he'd tucked away at the bottom. He then slipped them into the weathered, empty Amazon box marked "return" seated outside the library door.

He stepped inside and greeted Ms. Ornelas, the only school librarian in the entire world with a habit of talking louder than the students. She looked up from her messy desk and waved with a smile. Of course, Efrén smiled back as he headed toward the fiction area, second row, top shelf—the same exact spot he'd left off the last time he was here.

Without missing a beat, he began running his fingers along the spine of each book until something called to him. And something always did.

This time, his fingers paused over a teal book with orange letters. *The House on Mango Street*? He thought about Highland Street, about the fruit trees—and for a split second—wondered if this book might somehow be about his own neighborhood. He pictured little kids in diapers chasing chickens running around freely, while slightly older kids played school on the porch or made mud pies to share with the entire neighborhood. Yeah, right. Efrén scoffed at the idea.

"That's an amazing book," a voice said behind him.

It was Jennifer Huerta—the only other student who

checked out as many books as Efrén.

She stood beside him, her long, wavy hair held tightly in a braid. "It's about a girl named Esperanza trying to discover who she is and where she belongs in the world. It's my favorite book ever," Jennifer said, clutching a Lord of the Rings book to her chest.

Efrén's eyes went wide. "Really?"

"Yeah, the girl in it sounds a lot like me. Even uses Spanglish once in a while."

Efrén cringed. "My fifth-grade teacher, Mrs. O'Neal, used to get mad if we spoke that way in class."

"Why? What's it to her?"

Efrén liked this side of Jennifer. She had a bit of attitude he hadn't seen before.

"I don't know. Maybe because she couldn't understand what we were saying."

Jennifer's laugh surprised Efrén. They'd been in the same honors classes since last year and he'd never heard her laugh before.

"What's *your* favorite book?" she asked.

"Probably *Maniac Magee*."

"*Maniac Magee*? I haven't read that one."

"Yep. It's amazing. It's about this kid, stuck between

two different worlds that don't get along just because of the color of their skin. And at the end, he actually— sorry, don't want to spoil it for you."

"Oh, don't worry about me. I always read the endings first."

"Wait, what?"

"Yeah. I like to read the endings first. That way I know that there's a happy ending. Otherwise, the books are too suspenseful for me and I bite my fingernails until the tips begin to hurt." She laughed. "I'll probably have to wear gloves on the school's election day."

Efrén's mouth decided to betray him. "I'm sure you'll do great," he blurted out.

"Oh, thanks," Jennifer answered, a look of surprise on her face. "But I don't have my hopes up too high."

"So why are you running?"

"I was home watching a report on how undocumented families were being separated. They had kids in cages. Like animals. And that really hurt." She looked back at Efrén. "You ever buy eggs at the store?"

"Yeah. Sometimes, Amá sends me to the corner market whenever we're out."

"You ever notice the labels?"

Efrén shook his head.

"Most of the eggs say they come from cage-free chickens. Which means people in this country worry more about chickens than they do about undocumented children. It makes me feel so—"

Her eyes welled up and she stopped to look around and make sure nobody else was close enough to hear her. Then, with her head down, as if she was ashamed, she added: "Mi mamá no tiene papeles."

"Don't worry. My parents are here illegally too. I swear . . . I won't tell anyone."

Jennifer smiled ever so slightly. "I know you won't. That's why I told you. My mom says I'm a great judge of character. Says I'd make a great juez someday and I'll have my own courtroom." She reached into her backpack and held out a brown paper lunch bag. The words SOMOS SEMILLITAS were neatly written across the front.

"We are seeds? I don't get it."

"It's a Mexican saying. 'Nos quisieron enterrar, pero no sabían que éramos semillas.'"

Efrén rubbed his lower lip. "They tried to bury us . . . but they didn't know we were seeds?"

"Yeah. That's it. My mom likes to remind me of this *every* day. She's right though. That's why I'm running. Figured I could make a difference, even if just at school."

Efrén's smile widened. "I like it. I think your mom is right. You'd make a great politician."

She laughed. "Well, I think you'd make a great school president."

Efrén's cheeks turned bright red. "Thanks, but I'm just campaigning for David."

"Too bad. Losing wouldn't hurt as much if it were against someone like you."

Again, Efrén's mouth continued on autopilot. "I think *you'd* make a great president." Immediately, he covered his mouth with his hand.

Jennifer smiled and pulled her bright pink rolling backpack in close to her. "I better go," she said. "Han is waiting for me." But before leaving, she leaned in and gave him a quick hug before vanishing behind the next aisle.

Efrén directed his gleaming eyes back at the book in his hand. His ears perked up. *"We didn't always live on Mango Street."* He leaned up against the shelf and began reading the first page.

Jennifer was right. This book was different.

Efrén thought about all the different neighborhoods he'd lived in. There had been a lot. But Highland Street had eventually become his home, just like he imagined Mango Street had for the girl telling the story.

He read on. *"But even so, it's not the house we thought we'd get."*

He'd heard Apá say this very same thing many times. Efrén closed the book. He'd hit the jackpot today. There was no need to keep on searching.

Efrén looked at the time. Nutrition break was almost over, and he headed to the checkout desk where Ms. Ornelas sat with a big jug of coffee beside her as she repaired a torn page from a graphic novel.

"Hi, Ms. Ornelas."

"Oh, Efrén. How's my number one reader?"

Efrén shrugged. "Pretty good," he answered. He held up his book. "I'd like to check out this book."

She looked up. "Just one?"

"Yeah. Just one today."

At lunchtime, Efrén's friends picked at their food, tossing out anything they couldn't coat with Tajín chili powder. After that, Efrén and Abraham jostled for a better position to watch David showing off his skills on his new Nintendo Switch, which he'd gotten a month ago for his birthday.

Both boys cringed with every strike from Charizard, as if it were them dueling it out.

If only Apá's boss had come through with the bonus he'd promised him for finishing a recent construction job early. Then, he would have been able to keep *his* promise and buy Efrén his own device. That dream, however, burst along with Apá's appendix. Not only did the bonus not happen, he also got fired from that job after taking too long to heal.

There was still a scar on his lower abdomen that Apá liked to call his zipper. Claimed it was where he kept his wallet and keys.

Efrén sat and watched as David claimed yet another victory.

"Don't worry, guys," said David. "When I become school president, I'm gonna return the Chromebooks they assign us and buy Switches for everyone instead."

Abraham turned and raised his hand high in the air. Efrén high-fived him back. *Like it could really be that easy*, he thought.

David shut the game off and slipped his device back

into his backpack. "You guys wanna help me after school?"

"Help with what?" asked Abraham, picking at a scab on his elbow.

"Make posters and flyers for the election."

"Sorry, I've got soccer practice. Our coach makes us run laps if we're late," Abraham said.

David's goofy grin vanished. "C'mon. How 'bout you, Efrén?"

"Well, since I did walk to school alone, I'm guessing it's all right if I stay late and walk home alone too. But I better leave my mom a message. Can I borrow your phone?"

David's grin reappeared as he handed over his phone. "Great. We'll start with the bathroom posters."

Efrén and Abraham turned to each other. "Bathroom?" they asked in perfect sync.

"Can you guys think of a better place?" He raised his arms as if he were spreading out an invisible set of plans. "I was thinking of placing one in each stall. Maybe even over the urinals."

Efrén closed his eyes and laughed.

An hour and a half later, after leaving a message for Amá, he and David were up to their elbows in paint.

The ASB leadership room was huge and had everything a future president elect could ever need: rolls of poster paper, glue, popsicle sticks, straws, markers, tempera paints, watercolors, foam, paintbrushes—even foam brushes.

Efrén ripped off another yard of yellow paper from the roll. "Are you sure about this?"

"Yeah. Haven't you ever heard of a word-of-mouth campaign? Once a few kids see our posters, they'll start telling their friends and, presto! Free publicity." David held out his completed poster.

Even with the uneven letters slanting to one side, the caricature at the center showed an uncanny similarity to Jennifer Huerta.

David pointed to the slogan beneath the drawing. "Check it out: DON'T GO NUMBER TWO. VOTE FOR DAVID AND GO NUMBER ONE! Dude, get it? Number two? Number one? The posters are gonna go inside of each stall door."

Efrén stood there, dumbstruck. "Well, I guess. If your goal is to get people talking, then yeah, why not?"

David's face lit up. "The only problem is, which one of us is gonna sneak into the girls' bath—"

"Not me!" exclaimed Efrén, cutting off his friend.

"You have to. Girls go in there in huge groups. And I need their votes. The future president can't be seen inside the girls' room. What would people say?"

Efrén was about to argue, but caught himself. What was the point? A best bud is a bud for life and Efrén wouldn't have it any other way.

"Fine. But you owe me, big time!"

Before long, Efrén found himself standing outside the girls' bathroom, a role of painter's tape hanging from his forearm. "There better be some awesome perks coming my way after you win."

David smiled and nodded, his head bouncing up and down.

Efrén searched the hallway for signs of anyone coming. No one. The coast was clear. "Well, here goes nothing."

The entranceway pretty much resembled that of the boys' restroom, minus the nasty smell of day-old pee. Efrén rounded the corner. "Whoa!" This bathroom was twice the size. Twice the number of sinks. Twice the number of stalls. "David! You wouldn't believe it in here. It actually smells clean."

"Dude, hurry. The after-school program usually

does a bathroom break about now."

Efrén hurried over to the handicap stall at the end. He opened the door and his eyes went wide at what he'd found inside. "Oh, man. You won't believe this!"

"Believe what?" asked David.

Efrén ran outside and grabbed David by the sleeve, practically pulling him out of his sneakers. "Come inside," he said, leading him to the furthest stall.

"This better be import—" David froze as Efrén held the door open. "No way! This was my idea."

An impressive caricature of David, drawn on yellow poster paper, hung over the toilet.

"Go Number One, vote Jennifer Huerta. Or go Number Two, and vote for David Warren." David pointed to the drawing. "Look at that nose! I look like that bird on the Froot Loops cereal."

Efrén did his best to stifle a chuckle.

David shook his head. "This is just wrong."

"But kind of funny, right?"

David let out a breath. "I'm gonna fix it." He reached into his backpack and rummaged through a mess of papers.

"What are you looking for?"

"Wite-Out. I'm gonna make the nose smaller."

"I don't know, dude. The bylaws say that messing with a person's campaign poster could get us disqualified."

"By-what?"

"Bylaws. The rules Ms. Salas went over. Remember?"

David's shoulders dropped. "Can I at least make the diamond earrings larger? I don't want people thinking I'm cheap too."

"You really think that—"

Without warning, David clamped his hand over Efrén's mouth. "Shh . . . I hear someone coming."

Both Efrén and David barricaded themselves inside the stall.

David whispered into Efrén's ear and pointed. "Our feet."

Efrén nodded and the boys squatted over the toilet seat, hands stretched along both walls for balance, ears wide open.

A stall door opened and slammed shut.

The boys stayed perfectly still, each holding his breath to keep quiet. But what came next was a surprise to both of them. It was a girl, crying.

"Come on," said David, gesturing with his hand.

The door creaked and the boys inched their way toward the door. But Efrén froze at the stall where the girl had entered. Under the door, he could see a bright pink rolling backpack—Jennifer's.

Efrén didn't know her too well, but this didn't stop him from wanting to knock on her door. But what could he say: "Hey, Jennifer, I was a few stalls away and couldn't help but notice you crying?"

David waved his arms frantically to get Efrén's attention.

There wasn't much for Efrén to do but follow David's lead.

It was about five o'clock by the time the two boys parted ways along Highland Street. David was on his way to the Boys & Girls Club for some sort of foosball tournament, while Efrén hurried home before Max ate both their shares of dinner.

Reaching under his collar, Efrén unfastened the key from the safety pin and let himself in. "Amá, I'm home!" He headed toward the restroom, the only other room in the studio apartment. "Sorry I'm late. I had to help David with his campaign posters." He knocked three times. Nothing. "Amá?"

He went in. No one was there. He scanned the kitchen table. There were no place mats or plates or any other sign that dinner had even been started. It wasn't like Amá to not cook, not with her dislike of eating out. She always said that you couldn't trust strangers to wash their hands before handling your food and that there was no sense in paying for something she could make cheaper—and better.

Maybe she'd taken the Minions down to the school playground to get the wiggles out of their system. Especially Max. He didn't do well in confined spaces.

The mattresses filled the living room space, which seemed odd because Amá usually lined them up against the wall during the day. Efrén shrugged. Maybe she'd forgotten. With a running start, he tucked his chin in and flipped onto the pile of mattresses. Finally, he could enjoy some peace and quiet. He reached into his backpack and pulled out his new library book.

Half a chapter in, hunger made his belly quake. Efrén got up and looked around. Strange. Very strange.

He opened the front door and felt a cold breeze coming in. *Hmm.* He scanned the pile of winter jackets behind the door. A different feeling now filled his stomach. Something was wrong. Amá never let anyone—including Apá—leave the house without a jacket if there was even a single gray cloud overhead.

Two steps at a time, Efrén zipped downstairs toward the school playground. The cold chill caught him off guard. He looked up at the setting sun and then around at the last of the neighborhood kids straggling home. Soon, the riffraff (or chusma, as Amá liked to call them) would begin trickling out, and it was best to try to avoid them.

Efrén picked up speed, stopping only as he approached the school's closed gate. He looked down at the heavy-duty padlock, his mind now doing sprints. Other than the food truck, corner market, and laundromat, there was nowhere else Amá could have gone.

He did a quick check of the playground, then raced back home. He stopped short of his front door and bent over, trying to catch his breath. That's when he discovered a paper caught in the metal screen door. He stuck his pinky finger between the metal designs and pushed the paper out. It was a note from Doña Chana, the Tupperware lady a few doors over. The slip read: *LA SRA. SOLOMON ME DEJÓ LOS NIÑOS. ESTÁN BIEN.*

It didn't make sense. Why would the little ones' teacher, Ms. Solomon, drop them off there? Amá should have picked them both up hours ago. With his heart thumping, Efrén bolted over.

However, before he could even knock on Doña Chana's front door, Max and Mía came rushing out, their arms outstretched. Max's itty-bitty arms wrapped tightly around Efrén's waist while Mía tried climbing up to hug him. As relieved as Efrén was to find the twins, the question still remained: Where was Amá?

The answer lay somewhere in Doña Chana's worried look. "Mijo, les hice un caldito de pollo bien rico. Por favor, entra."

A bowl of warm chicken soup sounded great. Normally, he would have politely waited for her to insist, but something about her voice made him nervous. There was something she wasn't telling him. "Sí, gracias," he said, determined on finding out what.

The inside of her studio was pretty much a mirror image of where Efrén lived. Only, instead of piled mattresses, the entire room was surrounded by stacked boxes. Doña Chana was on her way out; the only thing not packed was the television, which sat across a floral sofa bed that looked like it'd been picked off some highway curb.

Efrén, Max, and Mía crammed around a table so

small that it made the entire kitchen area feel much larger than theirs. Doña Chana reached into a box, pulling out a plastic spoon for each of them.

The soup was great. Maybe not Amá great, but enough to help calm his nerves. Enough to gather the courage to finally ask, "Doña Chana, where's my Amá?"

Instantly, her face tensed. "Max. Mía. ¿Por qué no se van a ver la televisión?" When it came to watching TV, they didn't need to be asked twice. That left Efrén alone with Doña Chana at the dinner table. Efrén braced himself.

"Mijo," Doña Chana said, her voice high and tortured, "tu mamá . . . she called. La migra la tiene. Los descarados de ICE la recojieron buscando trabajo en una fabrica."

Efrén's body chilled to its core. He'd heard the word "ICE" whenever someone brought up immigration—usually in the same way kids talked about El Cucuy, the Latino version of the boogeyman. He'd grown up hearing about it, fearing it.

It made sense to arrest bad people. But Amá? She'd never done *anything* wrong.

"¿Y Apá? Does he know?" Efrén asked.

"Not yet. He was out on a job. I left a message for him to call me." Doña Chana studied Efrén's pale face. "Mijo, everything is going to be okay."

Efrén turned toward his brother and sister and then back to Doña Chana. "We have to get her back."

Doña Chana's worried look returned. "Yes, claro que sí. Your father will get her back. You will see."

Efrén wanted to believe her. Only he kept thinking about the neighborhood gossip he'd picked up from a few of Amá's comadres at the communal laundromat—stories about nearby factories getting raided and somebody—usually someone's distant cousin—getting caught and deported. From what Efrén could gather, the word ICE wasn't something people liked to talk about—at least not around kids. He wondered what the comadres might say now. He imagined them blessing themselves, imploring la Virgen María and any of a long list of patron saints to pray for Amá's safe return.

Efrén turned his attention away from the yellowed apartment walls and watched Doña Chana tap her purple nails against the table. He had heard of Doña Chana's repeated attempts to stop smoking. The smell of smoke had apparently slowed her Tupperware sales.

Seemed people didn't want to buy items reeking of cig-arettes.

Now, she reached into her back pocket and pulled out a silver lighter.

Efrén was about to hold his breath when she reached for a glass candle from a kitchen cabinet with the image of some saint he didn't recognize. She placed the vela-dora down on the edge of the table.

Efrén watched her struggle with her lighter.

"Ay, qué cosa tan inútil," she said, getting up and struggling to light the candle over the stovetop.

*Useless . . .* That was exactly how Efrén felt.

# THREE

Although it didn't happen very often, Max and Mía were still awake when Apá returned from work. No matter what books Efrén read, or how many stories he told them, Max and Mía wouldn't go to sleep. Probably all the Pulparindo candy Doña Chana gave them.

Dressed in matching fleece onesies, they clamped onto each of his legs the second he entered the apartment. He looked up at Efrén, his lips pressed tight—a sure sign he had something important on his mind.

Apá tossed his heavy jacket and lunch pail onto the floor while trying to keep his balance.

"¡Ándale, burro!" Mía hollered, waving her arm in the air as Apá bounced his leg up and down.

"Now me." Max sat on Apá's other foot, calling for his turn. Apá took a deep breath and braced himself before playfully straining to lift Max off the floor.

"Ay, muchacho. ¿Qué tanto estás comiendo?"

Max's weight sent Apá tumbling down onto the mattress closest to the door. Everyone in the room laughed, all except Efrén, who sat alone at the table, waiting to talk with his dad.

Apá looked up, his face still covered with streaked dirt from where he'd wiped away sweat earlier. He exchanged a worried look with Efrén.

Having to chase work wherever he could find it, Apá did not get to spend much time with his family. But when he did, he made a point of spending as much time with them as possible.

Sometimes he and Efrén would kick a soccer ball around while Max and Mía went up and down the playground slide. Other times, when Apá's back was too sore to play—and Max and Mía let them—they'd pop a fresh batch of popcorn, plop themselves onto the mattresses, and watch a soccer game on TV.

But there'd be no playing today. Apá approached Efrén, tousling his hair and pulling him into a tight hug. "No te preocupes, hijo. Tu madre volverá. Te lo juro."

Efrén wanted to believe him and trust Apá would

find a way of bringing his mother back. Only Efrén couldn't think of a single person who'd been deported and made it back to the neighborhood.

And that scared him more than anything else.

"Apá," Mía said, walking up while shamelessly adjusting her underwear, "¿dónde está Amá?"

Again, Apá pressed his lips tightly together. "She went to visit your aunt Martha. She said she'd bring back some of that tamarindo candy you guys like so much."

The answer seemed to satisfy Mía's curiosity. Efrén wished it were that simple for him.

As much as the adults liked keeping kids in the dark, Efrén had heard enough. He knew about the raids happening around the country. Around the state. Around his city.

And there'd been other changes too. Take Apá, for example. Last summer, he'd made a point of coming home early on at least one day and taking the entire family to the beach. Max and Mía would stay seated exactly where the waves ended, and with plastic shovel and bucket, they'd work on creating the largest castles possible. Efrén would take his cheap Styrofoam boogie board, and ride each breaking wave until he ended up face to face with Max and Mía.

But over the last few months, Apá seemed to come up with all sorts of excuses not to take the family outside the neighborhood. And Efrén understood why. He'd heard about ICE setting up checkpoints and literally taking people off the streets. He'd heard about ICE helicopters scaring people out of their homes and hauling them away. He'd even heard of ICE making stops at Mexican-geared supermarkets and handcuffing anyone who couldn't prove they belonged. Whether the rumors were true or not, they sounded real enough to worry him.

And he wasn't the only one.

One time, Denny's was having a kids-eat-free deal, so Apá and Amá decided to treat the family to something special. But when they were escorted to a corner booth, Efrén could sense something was wrong. Both Apá and Amá looked nervous, jittery even. The reason was simple. There were two white officers seated directly across the aisle, each wearing khaki cargo pants and black shirts with the word "ICE" printed in giant, white letters.

And no matter how hard Apá or Amá tried hiding it, Efrén could sense their fear. And that was scary in itself. Apá was the strongest, bravest man he knew. And yet, he was no match against an entire country trying to get rid of him.

Apá looked over at Efrén and, as if he could read his mind, leaned over and kissed the top of his head before turning his attention back to the little ones. One at a time, he picked them up and swirled them about the room as if they were superheroes. Max extended his arms out in front of him, pretending to be Superman. Mía, on the other hand, waved a pretend mallet like her favorite Mexican TV hero, el Chapulín Colorado. But even this crimson grasshopper couldn't bring a smile to Efrén's face.

Efrén watched Max and Mía laughing, jealous of how clueless they were to what had happened. Part of him—a larger part than he'd like to admit—even wished he could be picked up and kept in the dark too.

Unfortunately, the only superhero he wanted to hear from was his own Soperwoman. And he wasn't sure how her ability to flip steaming tortillas with her bare hands was going to help get her home.

Efrén had hoped that Apá and he could talk once the little ones had settled into bed. To help speed up the process, he helped them with their prayers and then read from their favorite Dr. Seuss book *The Sneetches and Other Stories.*

Max and Mía rubbed their round bellies and chanted along with every single word. Two-and-a-half readings later, they were asleep.

On normal nights, Apá would come home, kiss the entire family, and head straight into the shower. But tonight, Apá took a seat at the table still wearing his muddy boots and jeans, silently staring at the phone while picking at the dead skin hanging off his weathered fingertips. Efrén took a seat beside him, unsure of what to say.

The thick silence broke as the house phone finally rang and Apá sprang off his chair.

Efrén stood and leaned in close to him, holding his breath in the hopes of hearing Amá's voice again.

It was Amá! Her words were muffled, but full of emotion. Efrén wanted to call out to her, but he didn't want to wake the twins. Instead, he forced himself back onto his chair and observed as Apá jotted down notes onto the back of a napkin.

"Sí. Sí entiendo." Even though his eyes told a different story, Apá's voice sounded strong and reassuring.

Finally, he turned back to Efrén, a rare smile appearing. "Sí, aquí está, escuchando." Apá held the phone out.

As much as he wanted to sound as confident as Apá, there was no overcoming the clump of emotion pinned to the back of his throat. "Amá . . ."—tears poured down his face—"where are you?"

She sniffled. "I'm fine, mijo."

Efrén wished he could believe her.

"Really, I'm fine," she insisted. "I'm getting released back into Mexico tomorrow. Don't worry about me. I'm thinking about going down to Ensenada, spending some time at the beach."

In spite of himself, Efrén laughed. He knew she hated the ocean. The smell of dead fish and the squawking of sea gulls. "But when will you be back?"

Amá took a moment to answer. "Soon. Very soon. But in the meantime, I need you to promise me one thing."

Efrén shut his eyes and nodded. "Sí, claro."

"I'm going to need you to look after your brother and sister, especially Max. You know the kind of trouble that boy gets into."

"No te preocupes de nada. I want you to enjoy your

time off. Work on your tan a bit."

Her voice now quivered as she laughed. "Efrén . . . te amo. Muchísimo."

"I know. I love you too."

He passed the phone back to his father, who continued writing down notes and making phone calls late into the night.

Efrén lay in bed awake, swatting away the occasional arm from his face. If only he could go to sleep and wake up to find that the entire day had been a bad dream. Then he could sit beside Amá at the breakfast table and tell her about David's decision to run for president, about all the crazy campaign promises and posters. Amá would laugh and shake her head, like she always did whenever she heard any of the crazy travesuras el Periquito Blanco dreamed up.

But there would be no laughter anytime soon. Not until his mother returned.

In the past, whenever Efrén found himself struggling to sleep, he'd simply roll off his mattress and climb up beside her. Somehow, no matter the time, she'd always sense his presence and wrap her arms around him. And then on cue, she'd say a short prayer before running her fingers along his hair, piojito style. She called it that because it mimicked the technique she'd used to delouse the twins after their first month of kindergarten.

Her fingers were magical—good for much more than flipping tortillas. They were warm and soothing, to the point that anyone under their care would slip into a restful sleep in minutes. Even Apá was not immune to their power.

But there would be no piojitos tonight.

That night, Efrén lay in bed watching Apá toss and turn. Like their light cajeta-brown hair and crooked smiles, they now had this in common too.

Efrén tried distracting his mind with positive thoughts, but all the positivity he could muster was the fact that he positively missed his mother.

# FOUR

Efrén awoke to a gentle tug on his shoulder. He didn't know when he'd eventually fallen asleep, but by the way that his eyelids weighed heavily, he knew it hadn't been that long. "Maxie," he said, "you can go to the bathroom on your own. I need to sleep."

"Mijo, despierta," Apá whispered. "Wake up."

Efrén forced his eyes open and sat up. His father was dressed, ready for work in a clean version of what he'd worn the night before.

"I'm leaving for work early. I asked Doña Chana if she might take you and your hermanitos to school today, maybe keep an eye on you afterward. Only she can't. Has a Tupperware shipment to pick up in LA."

"It's okay, Apá," Efrén said, rubbing away at the sleep in his eyes. "I can get them dressed, and fed, *and* take them to school myself."

"Are you sure, mijo? What about Max—you know how difficult Max can be."

"He's fine. I can always bribe him with food. "Really, it's no problem."

Apá chuckled. "All right. Here." He reached into his pocket and pulled out a twenty-dollar bill. "I'm going to need you to go to the troquita and pick up some food for dinner. Just don't bribe him with soda or he'll never go to sleep."

Efrén took the money and slipped it into his underwear waistband. "Don't worry about us." He turned to check that the little ones were still asleep. "Just get Amá back."

Apá nodded. "A friend at work knows a guy who works as a coyote. He might be able to get her across really soon . . . if I can wire the money in time."

"Do we have enough money?"

"Almost. But my same friend is lending me the rest of the money we need." Again, Apá smiled with his mouth closed tightly. Efrén could see the worry on his face. "Now, mijo, get some more sleep. I left the alarm set for you."

"It's okay. I don't think I'll need it." He was too nervous to sleep.

By the time the alarm finally did go off, Efrén was already in the kitchen trying to figure out what to feed Max and Mía. Amá had this thing about not having her kids eating the school breakfasts. "Too much sugar and preservatives," she'd say.

Efrén stared into the refrigerator. What could he possibly do with one egg, a strip of ham, pickles (which only Apá liked), a packet of biscuits, and the three or four swigs of milk left?

If Amá were here, she'd roll up her sleeves and wave her wooden spoon and make a milagro happen.

The pressure was on. He opened the top cabinet and found a container of cinnamon and sugar. He turned to the bottle of oil and smiled.

A bit later, Efrén and Max and Mía stood along the kitchen table, forming the premade biscuit dough into misshapen animal figures.

"Okay. Now stand back, you two. The oil is very, very hot. Last thing I want is Amá coming home to a pair of charred twins."

Max and Mía got the hint and decided to wait behind the balcony curtains.

"On three. One. Two. Three." Efrén plopped the first animal biscuit into the oil, causing a splash that crossed over half the stovetop.

"Is it working? Are we really having donut critters?" asked Max, his eyes barely visible behind the curtain.

Efrén leaned in and watched the dough sizzle. "I'm not sure it's supposed to cook this fast." He reached in with the spoon and tried flipping it over, but the doughy critter flopped right off the pan and onto the kitchen floor.

Max and Mía both shrieked.

Like a good big brother, Efrén rushed in and scooped up the tiny beast. "Don't worry! I'll just rinse it." Again, both hermanitos stood back and watched.

"See?" Efrén said, holding the soggy half-cooked donut thingy. He returned to the stovetop and flung the critter back into the oil. The pan erupted. Oil jumped everywhere, even onto the back of his hand. Efrén yelped and ran his hand under cold water. Max and Mía shrieked again, only much, much louder.

A half hour later, Efrén found himself at the elementary school lunch tables, eating generic Cheerios with his brother and sister.

"Hey, guys," Efrén said, soaking his burn inside a milk carton, "how about we *not* mention any of this to Apá, yeah?"

# FiVE

With the little ones now under Ms. Solomon's care, Efrén suddenly remembered his homework—which he'd completely forgotten about until that very minute.

Huffing and puffing, he finally reached the middle school. He needed to get to the library and do his homework if he hoped to keep his perfect year-and-a-half streak of not missing a single assignment. But as he pulled out his class agenda, he discovered three different tasks waiting for him. He scanned the math worksheet. It was simple enough; he could finish it during the warm-up activity at the start of class. Same with the Venn diagram on amphibians for science. But how could he annotate an entire three-page article for Mr. Garrett with only fifteen minutes until the first bell?

Efrén's mouth went sour and his stomach tightened.

It wasn't as if Mr. Garrett would understand. No way. Not him. Not unless . . .

Mr. Garrett had a simple policy. NO HOMEWORK EXTENSIONS! At least not without a parent's note.

But the only way to come up with one would be to . . .

Efrén shook his head as if trying to throw the idea away, but it held strong.

He gathered his belongings and headed to the cafeteria. David liked cutting it close, so chances were he might not be there. *Still*, Efrén thought, *it was worth checking*. If he were on time for a change, he'd no doubt be at the lunch area, munching on anything cheese flavored.

Efrén hurried down the stairway. Finding his best friend turned out to be pretty simple. All he had to do was look right ahead at the brightly dressed kid standing on top of a lunch bench, hollering something about doing away with all homework if he were elected president.

David leaped right off the table the second he caught sight of Efrén. "Yo, F-mon! It's working. Everyone I talk to is promising to vote for me. I'm telling you, it's in the bag."

Efrén leaned in close to examine David's lilac shirt and squinted, pretending to be blinded by its brightness. "What's up with the shirt?"

"It's the perfect blend of blue and pink."

"And?"

David rolled his eyes. "Simple. I want to appeal to all my voters. Blue for boys? Pink for girls?"

Efrén shrugged. "At least you'll be safe crossing the street."

"You want to help me pass out some flyers?"

Efrén caught himself pressing his lips together like Apá often did and felt the pressure building inside. "Actually"—he couldn't believe the words coming out of his mouth—"I need a favor."

"Anything, bro. Just name it."

The classroom door was ajar, yet every student in Mr. Garrett's first period class preferred to wait outside in the cold morning air.

Efrén poked his head inside. "Mr. Garrett?" asked Efrén. "May I please speak with you?"

Mr. Garrett lowered his magazine. "Mr. Nava, you do realize the bell has not yet rung?"

As Efrén took a deep breath, his eyes glanced over to Mr. Garrett's left hand. To his bare ring finger. There was no wedding ring. Just a white tan line in its place. According to the chisme at school, Mr. Garrett went through a tough divorce—even lost custody of his son and daughter. Probably the reason he was so cranky.

"I know, sir," Efrén said. "It's about my homework. I didn't get a chance to complete it."

Mr. Garrett's right eyebrow bent kind of funny. "You? Really? Guess that just leaves Jennifer Huerta for the perfect homework award at the end of the year. Unless, of course, you have a note."

Efrén dug his hand into his pocket and pinched at the corner of his phony note. He thought back to the Awards Night last school year, remembering how loudly both Amá and Apá had cheered when the principal called his name. Then, he imagined the look of disappointment on their faces if they ever found out what he'd done. He took his hand out of his pocket and clenched it closed. "No, sir. I don't have a note."

"In that case, go ahead and fill out a parent-notification slip and sign the missed homework log."

Efrén turned away, head down.

"Oh, and make sure you return the slip, or it's an automatic referral to the office."

*Office?* The word alone made him uneasy.

For the rest of class, Efrén did his best to stay focused as Mr. Garrett droned on about the lack of proper citations in today's media—well, as best as he could, with David slipping him little notes with campaign slogan ideas.

He watched the clock's minute hand inch its way through a complete loop.

Efrén thought about Apá's promise. Amá would be returning today. That was all that mattered. No more struggling to untangle Mía's long, wavy hair and figuring out how to braid it perfectly centered down her back. It also meant not having to chase a naked Max around the apartment, trying to put a fresh pair of undies on him.

Instead, it meant Efrén could go back to hiding out in the bathtub, finishing what could possibly become his favorite book—the whole time knowing that a delicious breakfast awaited him when he stepped out.

He took a deep breath—imagining the scent of cinnamon escaping a fresh pot of arroz con leche. The thought made his stomach growl.

Efrén sprinted home right after school, stopping only when he reached the bottom steps to his apartment. Gasping for breath, he eyed the closed blinds to his living room window. His initial thought was that Amá was not home, but he wasn't ready to accept defeat—not just yet. After all, it was completely possible that she was just tired from the difficult trip and decided to take a nap.

Efrén climbed the stairs, removed the key safety pinned onto the inside of his shirt collar. He unlocked both the metal screen and front door. Once inside, he searched each section of the room. The sheets over the mattresses lay unfolded, just as he'd left them this morning.

The only other place left to check was the bathroom, which he immediately headed to. He knocked and pushed the door open. Nothing.

He rushed into the kitchen area and searched the countertop for signs of his mother's cooking, perhaps the scent of salsa roasting on her comal griddle. But all he smelled was the stale scent of dread now filling the room.

Efrén rushed outside, where Doña Chana immediately waved him over.

"Oh, hi. I thought you were in LA."

"I was, but gracias a Dios . . . I came back early."

*Gracias a Dios?* Something was definitely wrong.

Efrén's stomach knotted up as he entered Doña Chana's apartment. The twins sat on the couch watching a cartoon on her cell phone.

This time, only Mía ran up to meet him. He boosted her up and gave her a long, sturdy hug. Though Mía couldn't understand the real reason behind it, she didn't mind at all. Mía planted her chin over his shoulder—a perfect fit. "When is Amá coming back?" she asked.

Efrén gazed up at Doña Chana, who looked on the verge of tears. She would stay that way the rest of the evening—barely speaking a word.

He pulled Mía back and smiled as big as he could. "Soon, Mía. Very soon."

That night, after about an hour of reading together, Efrén, Mía, and Max finally fell asleep. But soon, the sound of work boots entering the room woke up Efrén. He kept himself perfectly still, but his eyes followed as Apá made a beeline for the kitchen phone.

"No. No sé. ¿Qué puedo hacer?" Apá whispered to some mystery person at the other end.

Efrén couldn't believe his ears. Hearing Apá admit that he didn't know what to do next terrified him. There were so many things that could have gone wrong. According to laundromat gossip he'd heard bits of, crossing over was very dangerous. The smugglers, or coyotes, were not good people. They were criminals who took advantage of desperate families—sometimes just dumping them in the desert.

Apá sniffled and pounded the table hard. "No, le robaron su bolsa con todo su dinero. ¡TODO! Incluso el dinero que pedí prestado."

Wanting to catch every word his father said, Efrén stayed perfectly still and even held his breath. But hearing that Amá's purse had been stolen along with the money Apá had borrowed made Efrén's entire body shake.

"Ahora, ¿cómo consigo más dinero para cruzarla?" *Where would he find the money to get her home?* The question ripped a hole in Efrén's heart, even as more questions filled his mind.

Where could Amá be?

Was she hurt?

Was she scared?

Would she ever be coming back?

It was all too much for Efrén. He opened his eyes and pushed himself up. "Is Amá all right?"

"Sí. Sí. Hablaremos más tarde." Apá put down the phone and thumbed the corners of his eyes. "YES, mijo. She is fine."

"But she isn't coming home, is she?"

Apá rushed to Efrén's side and knelt by the mattress. "Son . . . look at me. It is just a delay. Nothing more. I swear."

Efrén squeezed his eyes shut, but no matter how much he tried to stop them, tears managed to seep down his face.

"It's okay to cry. I miss her too."

That was all the permission Efrén needed. He leapt into his father's arms, tucking his face into his chest.

Apá's own sobbing caused his body to bob up and down as if he were hiccuping. Efrén couldn't remember ever seeing his father cry like this. Not because Apá was too macho for something like that. Not Apá. If anything, he simply didn't want to add to the family's problems—like when he got sick last month and Amá had to force him to stay home from work.

Despite his burning temperature, Apá insisted doctors were all quacks and that all they ever do is suggest

Tylenol, rest, and plenty of water. It wasn't until Amá raised her voice and scolded him about the poor example he was setting for his children that she finally got him to admit the truth: that he didn't want to spend the Christmas money he'd set aside for the family on himself.

"Besides," he had said, pointing to his so-called zipper on his belly, "I'm still paying for this visit, remember?" Amá didn't laugh. As it turned out, the doctor found Apá had pneumonia, something Amá blamed on the long hours he spent working in the cold.

Apá was tough as nails. Seeing him cry like this meant things were really bad.

And it scared Efrén. Scared him a lot.

# SIX

Saturday mornings had always been special for Efrén. It was a day he could sleep in just a tiny bit longer. A day he could expect a steaming bowl of arroz con leche and a freshly baked bolillo loaf waiting for him when he awoke. Then he could go into his study, which doubled as the bathtub, hurry through any homework he had, and stay until he finished a whole book or until Max or Mía needed to go potty—whichever came first.

However, this entire weekend went differently. With Apá working overtime, every single moment was spent making sure Max and Mía stayed busy enough that they wouldn't have time to miss Amá. It was something that required a lot from Efrén.

A lot of horsey rides around the apartment.

A lot of time pushing the twins back and forth on the school swing sets.

A lot of coloring.

A lot of time hiding and seeking.

A lot of everything.

So when Monday morning finally came around, Efrén didn't complain. In fact, he looked forward to the rest.

Unfortunately, Monday morning didn't exactly work out that way. Max was having a rough time, making the simple job of getting him dressed much, much more difficult.

"Come on, Maxie. You don't want to go to school in your underwear, do you?"

Max crawled out from under his blankets, causing a sigh of relief from his big brother.

"Okay, better." Efrén held the pair of pint-sized pants for him to step into. Only Max's plans were different. He threaded his pudgy arms through the pant legs until his hands peeked out from the other side.

"No seas payaso. Please, put them on right now."

Max pulled the arms out, only to stick his head in their place.

Efrén took a deep breath and massaged the sides of his forehead. He glanced over at the empty mattress beside him, trying to figure out what Amá would do.

Efrén looked straight into Max's penny-like eyes. "How 'bout this? If you get dressed, I promise to give you a horsey ride all the way to school."

Max shook his head no.

"How about . . ."—a crooked grin sprouted on Efrén's face—"I let you wear your Superman pajamas to school?"

Max nodded. It wouldn't be the first time Max went to school in pajamas—Ms. Solomon would understand.

Mía tugged at Efrén's shirt. "What about me? Can I go in pajamas too?"

Efrén bent down to look at her. "Sure . . . why not?" Having Max and Mía show up to school in pj's was the least of his worries.

Four days without Amá and already Efrén's world was starting to fall apart. By the time he reached school, the late bell had already rung. He hoped to see someone else, even a teacher, walking in late as well—but the campus hallways were empty. Even David had apparently made it to class on time.

The second Efrén entered the room, Mr. Garrett turned; his bushy eyebrows shot up in disbelief.

"Mr. Nava. You're late."

Efrén lowered his head and signed the tardy clipboard nailed to the wall. He'd seen Mr. Garrett belittle everyone who'd ever tried justifying being late. "Excuses," Mr. Garrett would say, "are like armpits. We all have them, and they stink."

So under the section of the form labeled *reason*, Efrén decided he was better off scribbling in the word "unexcused."

It felt like the whole class sat up, paying sharp attention when Mr. Garrett approached the center of the room. "Mr. Nava, this makes two infractions in a row. Is there something I should know?"

Efrén tried lifting his head and making eye contact like Amá had taught him to do with grown-ups, but the best he could do was shake his head. *Besides . . .* Efrén thought, *it won't make a difference.*

"Well, then . . . Mr. Nava, why don't you take a seat? And don't forget, this second infraction now means you have detention after school."

After school? There was no way. There was nobody else to pick up Max or Mía. Doña Chana had been scheduled to return to Guatemala that morning—some emergency with her parents.

Efrén stood frozen by the tardy clipboard, wondering how much, if any, of the truth he should tell Mr. Garrett. After all, he was a teacher. And according to Apá, teachers could never know about the family's legal status. Efrén remembered Apá telling him about the time the state voters passed a law that would have forced all teachers—even nice ones like Ms. Solomon—to report any undocumented kids to the authorities.

Apá, of course, held a grudge, saying that even though the courts erased the law, the masses had spoken and revealed exactly how they felt.

So even though Efrén was a US citizen, his parents were not, and he could not say a word about that.

"Mr. Nava? Is something wrong? Did you misplace your seat?"

"No, sir. I . . . I was . . . just—never mind."

And just like that, Mr. Garrett launched into a drawn-out explanation of how direct quotes were going to empower everyone's essay arguments.

Later, as the next bell rang, he reminded the class that paraphrasing would be coming next. But Efrén barely listened. It wasn't like him to disobey a teacher, but what could he do? He couldn't stay after school. And he couldn't tell the truth.

Efrén missed the old days, back when his neighborhood block made up his entire world, back when all he worried about was whether to play it safe with a game of marbles or brave a match of chicken fights along the monkey bars. It was all he thought about most of the day.

In seventh period, Mrs. Flores—the science teacher—had the entire class performing virtual dissections on worms. Efrén rushed through the lesson on account of Max and Mía. And when school finally let out, it was him leading the stream of kids off campus. More and more of them broke off into different neighborhoods with each block they passed. Those who veered off first lived in the fancy Floral Park block.

Those who were slightly less well-off disappeared into Washington Square, and so forth. So forth was where Efrén headed, right into Highland Street where apartment buildings and fruit trees made up most of the neighborhood. Reaching his block, he cut into the elementary school's parking lot. There, in the middle of the kindergarten courtyard, stood Ms. Solomon blowing her whistle at cars blocking the entrance.

"Efrén!" she called him over.

He walked into a big hug. "Hi, Ms. Solomon. Have you seen Max and Mía?"

"Over by the benches. I had a bit of trouble with them today. Where is your—oh, my God! Did your mom get the job?"

Efrén crinkled his face. "Job?"

Ms. Solomon held her hand up at a car. "Yes, the other day, she told me she was going over to Irvine for a job interview at a new company that makes high-end women's clothing. Said it was for a supervisor's position."

Efrén's mind raced. *That must have been when Amá got picked up.* As much as it bothered him to lie to Ms. Solomon, he didn't have a choice. "Yes, she started today. Says her boss is nice and that the pay is really good."

Ms. Solomon paused, making Efrén nervous. He couldn't help but wonder if she might be reading his face. After all, she'd known him since he was in her kindergarten class.

"Well, tell her I am so glad. Oh, and about Max and Mía . . . they seem a bit emotional—especially Max."

Efrén's mind went into a panic. Fearful of saying the

wrong thing, he simply shrugged instead.

"Well, maybe it was just an off day," she said, waving another car through. "And be sure to thank your mom for her mole recipe. Tell her that the dinner was a real success, thanks to her."

"Sure thing, Ms. Solomon."

With that, he walked over to the play area and took a seat on a bench, watching Max push Mía on a swing before leaping onto her lap. Mía didn't seem to mind one bit. Sometimes insufferable, always inseparable— like Ms. Solomon would joke. Efrén couldn't imagine telling them about what had happened to Amá. But how long could he keep the truth from them?

He looked over at the clock hanging over the bathrooms. Three o'clock. He'd have to start thinking about what to feed them. He headed over to join Max and Mía. Just as he started pushing them back and forth on the swings, a thought crossed his mind. *If Amá isn't able to come back home, does that mean we might have to go to her? Will we be forced to leave too?*

Efrén felt a tug at his side.

"I'm hungry." It was Max, right on schedule.

"Yeah, me too," called out Mía.

All the running around made the twins hungry. Now

more than ever, Efrén needed to stretch his money. Every dollar saved meant a step closer to getting Amá back.

Fortunately, Don Tapatío's food truck was a real bargain. But he'd have to be careful. Not everything there was cheap. He thought about the menu, crunching numbers in his head.

Carne asada tacos were definitely the best bargain. They were small but came with double tortillas. Efrén could take half the meat and turn each taco into two—a milagro of his own.

"Maxie, Mía, how about some tacos?"

Max shrugged. He was easy—ate just about anything placed in front of him. It was Mía who Efrén needed to worry about.

"So, Mía? Tacos okay?"

"No. I want some of Amá's frijolitos with queso."

This very mention of their mother set Max off. "When is Amá coming back?"

"Soon," answered Efrén. "Soon."

"You're a mentiroso," Mía said, digging her finger into Efrén's belly. "You said she'd be back yesterday. You lied."

Mía was right. He had lied. Worse, he would have to

look the twins in the eye and do it again.

"The truth is that her sister, Tía Martha got sick. Amá is with her, making sure she gets better."

Mía rested her hands on her hip and squinted up at Efrén. "How do we know it's not a lie?"

Efrén held out his pinky finger. Mía smiled and hooked her finger around his.

"What 'bout me?" Max asked, holding up a chubby finger of his own.

Efrén offered his other pinky. "I swear, Amá will be back soon."

With that, Efrén stopped by Don Tapatío's food truck and fed the twins and himself. Using only six dollars, he turned three carne asada tacos into six and still managed to provide Mía the side of beans and cheese she wanted. If only he could find a way of getting Amá back home.

# SEVEN

During bath time, Max had demanded a game of battleship while Mía reenacted the entire plot of *The Little Mermaid*. Too bad for Efrén, both games called for a whole lot of splashing. By the time Efrén got them into bed, he was as beat as he was soaked.

With the twins now asleep, he headed to the kitchen table to start the hour or so's worth of homework waiting for him. But instead, Efrén pushed the thought of his assignments aside. He looked around at the apartment, thinking about the homes he passed each day to and from school. He thought about the grassy front yards large enough to play soccer in. He tried to picture himself running around like he'd seen the other kids at his school doing. Only, no matter how hard he tried, he couldn't seem to do it. His mind simply refused.

"Why?" it said. "What's the point? You're never going to have anything even close to that. Not you."

Efrén shut his eyes and took a deep breath, trying to fight the churning feeling in his gut. He missed Amá. Her smile. Her laugh. Her cooking and her hugs. But what he really missed was the way she seemed to brighten the entire world.

Now that she was gone, his life felt . . . well, secondhand.

He scanned the entire studio apartment, looked up at the water-damaged ceiling, then at the mismatched pieces of furniture that littered the room—and of course, down at the two twin mattresses covering most of the floor. Never before had his home felt so small, so poor.

His family didn't have much, but somehow, Amá had managed to keep this fact from really sinking in. Now, it would become his job to protect Max and Mía.

But how?

He unzipped his backpack and organized the assignments by degree of difficulty. Easiest first.

He stared at the sample sentence for language arts. *Sally's mother bakes wonderful cookies.* "Mother" was the subject, "bakes" was the verb, and "cookies" was the direct object. He turned to the kitchen and wondered if Amá would ever come back. Ever step foot in this kitchen again.

Just then, he heard the rattling of keys and then the metal screen to the front door creak open. *Apá!*

Efrén greeted him with a hug. Apá squeezed back, holding on a bit longer than usual. "Here," he said, handing him a pizza box. "Put this in the fridge. It's for the three of you, tomorrow." Apá turned toward the door. "I'll be right back."

*Pizza!* Max and Mía were going to be excited. Efrén peeked inside the box. *Pepperoni and pineapple!* His favorite.

He approached the window and saw Apá talking to a man. They were standing at the back of Apá's pickup truck. The man wore jeans and boots like Apá and said something that made Apá shake his head. Then Apá said something to make the man nod before offering his hand.

Then two men climbed onto the back of the truck and unfastened the metal tool bin.

*Apá's tools?* Efrén couldn't believe it. They were Apá's prize possession. No matter how much he used them, he always kept them looking new. Amá would sometimes joke, calling the collection his fourth child.

Not wanting to seem nosy, or meticbe, as Amá would say, Efrén decided to get back to his homework.

Apá entered holding a check in his hand.

Efrén couldn't help himself. "Is that enough money to get Amá back?"

"No. But it's a start." Apá looked over at the twins. "That's what we need to talk about. I landed an over-time job at my boss's headquarters, only it's late at night. So I need to know if you can handle the little ones a bit longer."

Efrén tried to make sense of what he'd just heard. "Yeah, but—wait, how are you going to work day and night? When will you sleep?"

"It's only temporary. Besides"—Apá flexed his biceps—"your old man is made of steel. You don't need to a worry about me, okay, mijo? I'll be working as a súper for a cleaning crew. They'll be doing most of the work. I'll just be supervising."

Apá went over to a drawer in the kitchen area and came back with a bagful of coins. *Amá's stash of laundromat money.* "Here. For food." He handed the coins to Efrén. "Between this and the check I just got, we'll be fine. Now get to bed. It's late."

Efrén wrapped himself in his blanket and watched Apá spray on some deodorant, then grab a slice of cold pizza and head off to work.

Apá was super too. A real Soperman.

The next day, after dropping off the twins, Efrén hurried to class. The first bell rang, but he waited by the door, watching the other students enter. What was he going to tell Mr. Garrett about having missed detention?

"F-mon? Whatcha doin'?" It was David, riding in on his skateboard while bouncing to a reggae beat that only he could hear.

Efrén shrugged. "Enjoying the last minutes of my life."

"What do you mean?"

"I didn't show up for detention yesterday." Efrén sighed.

David picked up his board. "Oh, wow. How 'bout I go in with you? He might yell at me for bringing in my skateboard and forget all about it. Come on."

Like most of David's plans, this one didn't work out either. Efrén entered the classroom. Mr. Garrett rose to his feet, looked up at the clock, and waited for the bell before saying a word.

"Mr. Nava. Do you mind explaining why you chose to disregard your detention yesterday?"

Efrén's stomach twisted, and—for a tiny moment—he thought he might be sick. He took a deep breath.

But Mr. Garrett would not let up. "Mr. Nava. I'm waiting."

Efrén's blood boiled. After everything he'd been through, now *this*? He looked up at Mr. Garrett and glared. "Why?" he said, his anger spilling out. "It's not like you even care."

The class went silent. Students looked around, mouths agape—total disbelief.

Efrén's chest rose and fell. All he could do was dig his nails into his palm.

Mr. Garrett's stood there, perfectly still, perfectly silent. He eyed Efrén's closed fists, wrinkly clothes, and sloppy, uncombed hair.

Efrén felt the room shrink and tugged at his shirt uncomfortably.

Strangely, though, Mr. Garrett's scowl seemed to lessen. Perhaps he'd just come up with the perfect consequence for him.

"Why don't you take a seat, Efrén?"

The class stirred once more. Not only had Efrén

talked back, Mr. Garrett had actually let it go. Heck, he had even addressed Efrén by his first name. That simply never happened.

Efrén took a seat, aware that all eyes were now on him.

Mr. Garrett's icy teacher voice suddenly returned. "Now, class, let's begin."

A half hour later, Mr. Garrett had completely filled out the whiteboard with a giant timeline of World War II. "Okay, now that I've gone over the material, go ahead and jot down the notes, silently."

Efrén couldn't explain what had happened. When class finally ended, he gathered his things and started walking out, but sure enough Mr. Garrett called him over. Efrén walked back to the teacher's desk, but Mr. Garrett didn't say a word, just stood, waiting for the last student to exit.

"Missed homework. Showing up late. Talking back. This lack of responsibility is so unlike you," he finally said. "Is everything all right?"

Efrén didn't answer. The safest thing for him was to keep his head down and shut his eyes tight enough to keep the tears from escaping.

Mr. Garrett's voice softened. "We adults can be pretty nearsighted sometimes. We forget that kids can have problems too. I mean, you normally come to class, ready to learn. And your clothes—I've never seen you without perfectly creased lines before."

Efrén's thoughts turned to Amá, and before he could pull his hand out of his pocket and wipe his face, a few tears managed to escape.

"I know what it's like to have one's life turned upside down." He turned to a frame on his desk, at a picture of his ex-wife and two kids. Then back at Efrén. "You, my friend, have that same look."

Efrén brushed his face with the fold of his sleeve and looked up at the photo. Mr. Garrett's ex-wife had long, wavy hair, a honey-beige complexion, and caramel eyes . . . just like Amá.

*A Latina? He'd married a Latina!*

*Did this mean he could now trust Mr. Garrett?* After all, the last thing he wanted to do was put Apá in danger too. If he were arrested, the entire family would most likely be uprooted like some uninvited weed and discarded across the border.

Mr. Garrett's brow crinkled as he studied Efrén's face. "Look, Efrén, you don't have to tell me what's going on with you, but you might want to consider telling someone you can trust."

Efrén's eyes panned from Mr. Garrett and back to the photo of his ex-wife and two kids. A boy and girl. For Efrén, it was now or never. "My mom . . . she got deported." The words seemed to escape alongside his rogue tears.

Mr. Garrett sighed deeply. "I'm so sorry to hear that. What about your father?"

"He's trying to figure out how to bring her back."

Mr. Garrett took another deep breath. "Listen, I'm not saying it will be easy, but you need to leave this up to your father. You're just a kid, and this is too much for you to place on your shoulders. Trust your father. Let him handle this, okay?"

Efrén wanted to accept what his teacher had said, but thoughts of Max and Mía immediately filled his head. Who would protect them while Apá was trying to get Amá back?

No. Efrén was the oldest. Amá's being deported was his problem too. He would need to help out every way he could—no matter what.

"Thank you, sir," said Efrén.

Mr. Garrett squeezed his eyes shut and sighed. "I just wish I could do more."

Efrén reached for the back of his neck and rubbed it. The worry. The pressure. They were wearing him down so much that he barely made it through math class. After solving Ms. Covey's latest math brainteaser, he reached for the duct tape wallet Apá had made for him and pulled out the money he had left over from the food truck the night before.

He patted his pocket, making sure he still had Amá's laundromat money.

The bell rang. Efrén joined the student stampede to the lunch line. He wasn't hungry but knew he couldn't afford to pass up a free meal, even if it was just a school lunch.

To be fair, the food the school served wasn't that bad, but it couldn't compete with the lunches Amá used to make for him each day. The burrito he picked up, just beans and yellow cheese, was greasy and runny—and yet, the corners of the flour tortilla somehow managed to stay hard and cold.

Efrén looked around at the side choices—the peanut

butter crackers, string cheese packets, and celery sticks—and wondered which items Max and Mía would most likely eat. *But what if the food is spoiled?* Efrén couldn't risk it and ended up going with the crackers and juice box.

Then, instead of joining up with David and the rest of his friends, Efrén took a seat at the far corner of the cafeteria. He spent most of the break staring at the clock overhead and carefully reorganizing the stuff in his backpack.

At 11:56 a.m., the afternoon supervisors took their positions along the stairway leading to the main floor. Lunch was about to end, and he needed to hurry. He scouted the area and headed toward an empty table.

Efrén's heart beat like a jackhammer. He knew that Amá's laundromat money wouldn't last long and needed to do something about it. Stealing food from school wasn't only wrong—it was embarrassing!

If any kids caught him, they'd never let him live it down. Regardless, Efrén knew what he needed to do. He unzipped his backpack and headed to the table closest to the main office. Kids didn't like to hang out around there. He leaned up against the closest trash bin and grabbed some of the unopened bags of celery and crackers students had thoughtlessly tossed away. Quickly, he zipped his bag shut.

"Hey, Efrén!" David called out as he ran over.

Efrén almost leaped out of his pants as he hid his backpack behind him.

"Where were you?" said David, as he walked over to him and extended his hand. Efrén reached over to him and the two did their usual dap, ending in a quick thumb-wrestling match.

Efrén hoped David wouldn't notice the trembling of his hands and voice. "Oh, just trying to come up with some new poster ideas . . . for your campaign."

"Yeah. I can't believe Jennifer stole my ideas. Anyway, come check this out. Some dude online actually drank a glass of milk through his nose. I swear!"

"Yeah, sure."

David grinned and rushed back to his table.

Efrén dropped his head and sighed. *How did things get this bad?*

# EiGHT

Later that night, the twins were busy turning over the mattresses and setting up a fortress while Efrén reheated the pizza over the comal, like Amá used to do. Only unlike her, Efrén used a pair of wooden tongs to turn each slice on the griddle. Because they were cold, the cheese did not stick.

"You two better clean up the mess you make. Got it?"

But Max and Mía were on their mattress, busy wrapping themselves inside the bedsheets.

Efrén scooped up the last slices and placed them each on a plate. He licked a dribble of red sauce off his finger and turned to watch the little ones twisting around in their fort—happy and worry free.

How much longer could he really keep them in the dark?

"All right, little burritos," he called, "go wash your hands and come eat."

Mía spun herself free and headed over to the counter. She stood on her tiptoes and peeked over. "What's for dinner?"

Efrén shrugged. "Grasshoppers and pasta, what else?"

Mía shot him a clear "yeah, right" look.

"Pizza. We're having pepperoni and pineapple pizza. So go wash up!"

Mía smiled and ran off, cheering.

Efrén opened the top cupboards and reached for Amá's favorite (and only) food platter. He then lined up the crackers and celery sticks he'd collected from school. "See, guys," Efrén said, "it's like a Sizzler buffet."

He'd have to pick up more supplies from school the next day or be forced to dig into the laundromat money for sure. Efrén looked down at the arrangement of food and felt shame over what he'd done. He tried pushing the feeling aside, tried reminding himself that taking food from the trash bin wasn't really stealing.

*Oh, Amá. If only you—*

The phone rang. A cold chill replaced the shame.

What if it was someone from ICE looking for Apá? What would he say? What if it was Apá? What if he was already in trouble?

Efrén reached for the phone. "Hello?"

A voice recording spoke: "Good evening, you have a collect phone call from"—Amá's voice then slipped in—"María Elena Nava"—then cut back to the recording. "Would you like to accept the charges?"

Efrén's heart raced. "YES. YES!"

"You are now connected."

It was strange, Efrén thought, Amá always managed to be there when he needed her. "Amá?"

"Sí, mijo. ¡Ay, cómo te extraño!"

"I miss you too," said Efrén.

"¿Cómo están los gemelos?"

"Max and Mía are both good."

"Is that Amá?" asked Max. Efrén turned around to discover the twins next to him, smiling from ear to ear.

"Yes," Efrén said, nodding. "Here, let me hit the speaker button."

"¡Hola, Amá!" hollered Max. "When are you coming home?"

"Pronto, mijo. Te lo juro."

That was a promise Efrén wished she could keep.

"¿Y tú, Mía?" asked Amá. "¿Estás ahí?"

Only Mía didn't answer when Amá asked for her.

Efrén covered the phone. "It's Amá. Say hi to her."

Mía crossed her arms and pursed her lips.

Efrén removed his hand from the phone. "I'm sorry, Mía's acting weird. You know how she gets."

"I'm mad at Amá!" she cried out. "For leaving us for so long."

"Mía!" Efrén shouted back.

"No. Está bien." Amá tried hiding her hurt. "Déjala. Es demasiado pequeña para entender."

She was right. Mía *was* too young to understand.

"Mira, Efrén," Amá added, "tell your Apá that I found a room. It's not much, but the owner is willing to wait for payment. Tell him that I will need some money soon. Okay?"

"Yes, Amá. I will."

"I have to go. I saw a help wanted poster at a drugstore nearby. My English didn't help me much in the US. Maybe here in Mexico, things will be different. Adiós, mijos. ¡Los quiero mucho!"

"We love you too. Right, guys?"

Max held his arms wide to show just how much.

"Adiós."

Efrén hadn't even set the phone down when he felt a kick at his shin. He looked over at Mía, who was winding up for a second attack.

"Why does Amá need to get a job? And why is she in Mexico?"

Mía's kick paled in comparison to the sting of her questions.

Efrén sighed. This was more of an Apá question. However, with him away working all night . . . it became one more thing Efrén would have to do. "Okay, okay. I'll tell you—the truth."

The meal was filled with firsts. It was the first time a warm slice of pizza ever sat untouched on Max's plate.

"So?" Mía asked, her eyes slightly squinted at her big brother.

Efrén's stomach cried out for a slice of pizza, but Mía was right. They needed to talk. "Okay. I'm sorry I didn't tell you two the truth before. Twice. I was just trying to keep you from worrying."

"Why?" asked Mía. "Did something bad happen?"

"Well, yeah. Amá got arrested."

Max's eyes went wide. "Arrested? What did she do?"

"No," Efrén clarified, "not really arrested, deported."

Max turned to Mía. "What's deported?"

Efrén took a breath. "It means that she was taken away."

"Why?" Mía demanded. "Who took her?"

"Immigration. ICE."

Mía shrugged.

"La migra," Efrén clarified. Finally, Mía seemed to understand.

Max wasn't so clear. "Did she do something wrong?"

"No, she didn't do anything wrong."

"Then why did they take her?"

"Because . . . she doesn't have permission to be here," said Efrén.

"Well, I give her permission."

"Yeah, me too," added Mía.

"No, not that kind of permission. She's not in this country legally."

"Wait," asked Mía, "so Amá did break a law?"

"No. Well, kind of, I guess. I don't know."

Max was more lost than ever. "So Amá's a criminal. Is she a spy?"

"No! Oh, geez." Efrén took a moment to gather himself. He looked around the room and caught a glimpse of the Dr. Seuss book on the floor. "It's kind of like that

Sneetches story," he explained. "Think of it this way: people in the United States have stars."

"'Upon thars'?" Max added.

"Yes, Maxie, 'upon thars.' And Amá, well, she doesn't have any."

Mía slammed her fist on the table. "But that doesn't matter. At the end of the book, nobody cares who has a star and who doesn't."

"I know," said Efrén. "I guess the world hasn't gotten that far yet."

The rest of the meal was spent in silence. No one ate. Not even Max. Efrén collected the untouched slices and saved them in the fridge. He turned on the TV and searched for their favorite shows. But even then, no one spoke a word.

Bedtime came a bit later than usual. Efrén's attempt to read from *The Sneetches and Other Stories* simply fueled more questions and, of course, more tantrums. Efrén offered Mía her naked plush doll, but she tossed it to the side. "No," she screamed. "I want Amá!"

Efrén searched the book bin for anything that didn't involve a mom character. In no time at all, he found an old favorite: *Clifford the Big Red Dog*.

Max and Mía each tugged at the book. "Careful or you'll tear it," warned Efrén, taking the book and raising it high above his head. "I'll read it to you . . . after you two get ready for bed."

Max leaped across the mattress and ducked under the sheets. Not Mía. She took her time.

"¿Listos? asked Efrén.

Both twins nodded.

Page after page, Max and Mía followed along.

"Again," called Max after Efrén closed the book.

Efrén pressed on his temples and rubbed his eyes. "Okay. One more time," he said before starting over.

"It wasn't until Max's head rested against Efrén—and Mía rested hers on him—that Efrén finally shut off the portable night-light.

Carefully, he slipped out from under Max's weight. He looked up at the clock, 9:35 p.m. Apá should have been home already. Efrén couldn't remember ever worrying about him like this. Apá was strong and always took care of the family.

Any time there was a strange noise outside, or the wail of sirens nearby, it was Apá who would get up to investigate. In Mexico, Apá had just made lieutenant in the police force before coming to the US, and often told Efrén stories about how he and his men took down some of the country's most powerful criminals, real drug traficantes. So having Apá around was like having a superhero watching over the neighborhood, protecting it from hoodlums who might cause problems. Even in nothing but boxers and black socks, Apá looked tough and fearless. Efrén couldn't imagine anyone wanting to mess with him.

Until now.

Standing up for his family in the neighborhood was one thing. Standing up against an entire country who wanted him gone was another.

Efrén went over to the window and peeked in between two of the broken blind slats. There, under a flickering streetlight stood Rafa and his crew, tailgating behind a souped-up Honda Civic.

Rafa wasn't a big guy. But he was as cool as he was skinny—bony, really. He had a huge smile and plenty of friends, especially little ones. That's because last summer, when the power went out and nobody had AC, he flagged over a paletero truck and bought every kid in the block ice cream.

Still, Amá didn't like him hanging out right outside their apartment.

Apá didn't like him at all. Said he attracted trouble.

And that's what Efrén feared when a black pickup truck approached with its high beams on. A few of Rafa's guys stepped forward with their hands reaching behind them.

Worried about what might happen next, Efrén held his breath. Fortunately, the shiny truck pulled alongside the guys and the driver lowered the windows, extending his hand to greet everyone. No doubt, he was part of the crew, there to show off his new ride. Efrén let out a breath and bent the slats back in place.

One thing he'd learned from helping Amá in the laundromat was that raids were sometimes announced online. He might be able to find some answers there. He reached for his school Chromebook. The house Wi-Fi signal was slow and unreliable, but at least it was theirs. Other kids at school had figured out an app to override passwords and get free access from the neighborhood, but Amá had always insisted on paying for their own account. It was just the way she was wired.

Not wanting to wake the twins up, Efrén took his internet browsing to the empty bathtub and did a search for ICE checkpoints in the area. Normally, reading in the tub was relaxing and fun. Not this time.

Search after search, he found "official" sites swearing that ICE did not conduct random checkpoints. Yet, he also found cell phone footage of ICE pulling people out of their cars and homes too.

Efrén chewed down on his fingernails. Any one of these men could easily be Apá. He clicked on another link. The screen immediately filled with headlines across the country. Images, articles, blogs, stories about undocumented immigrants—some positive, most not.

He clicked on articles—sometimes videos—of people being taken from the workplace, hospitals, even homes. Talk of a giant new wall came up repeatedly.

He could feel his insides begin to quake as his fear for Apá grew. Even with the extra hours, he shouldn't be this late.

Efrén was too tired, too unmotivated to do homework. He shut the computer and went back to bed, but instead of sleeping, he stared up at the textured ceiling. He followed the patterns until images began to form. At first, the images were simple, a set of eyes here, a smile there, but eventually the shapes became more elaborate.

His eyes followed a curved line beside an old water stain. A picture of a continent soon emerged: it was

North America, broken in half. He looked away for a second, but the image refused to disappear. Talk of "the wall" haunted him. He'd read a petition asking that the government strip citizenship from children of "illegal" immigrants, like Amá and Apá. His stomach twisted as he looked over at the front door, unsure if the police would one day come barging in to take them all away.

Just then, the sound of someone unlocking the front door sent Efrén's blood rushing. He knew the sound of Apá's keys jiggling, but he couldn't relax until he saw him crossing the doorway.

Apá came in carrying a grocery bag on a heavily wrapped hand. Efrén took the bag from him, his eyes glued to the red stain at the center of Apá's palm.

"Apá," he whisper-shouted. "¿Qué te pasó?"

Apá looked down at his hand and waved it dismissively. "Nada. Just a scratch."

Efrén panned up to Apá's puffy eyes. He had never seen his father look so tired. Efrén knew working construction without any rest was dangerous and didn't want to add to Apá's worries, but he also knew Amá's message was important.

Efrén walked over and watched as his father ran his injured hand under the kitchen faucet, watched the diluted blood seep down the slow-draining sink. "Amá called," he finally said.

Apá turned to him, forgetting all about his injury. "How is she? What did she say?"

"She said she was doing good. That she found a room . . . but will need money soon to pay for it."

Apá nodded while giving his hand a final rinse. "Don't worry, mijo. I will get it to her."

There was so much Efrén wanted to say. Questions he wanted to ask. But no, he couldn't bother Apá with questions now. Instead, he neatly put the groceries away.

In typical Apá style, he stripped down to his boxers and headed to the shower. The second the bathroom door shut, Efrén raced into the kitchen and began boiling water for a fresh cup of Nescafé like he'd seen Amá do plenty of times—something to help keep Apá awake during his new night shift. Efrén then headed toward the dirty clothes on the floor. They reeked of sweat and sawdust and felt stiff to the touch as he stuffed them into the laundry bag.

*Laundry!* Efrén felt his shoulders stiffen. He hated to spend the coins he had left, but knew he needed to go to the laundromat soon.

*No big deal. Separate the whites. Add soap. Dry and fold.*

"Mijo." Apá's voice caught him off guard. "I want you to take ten dollars out of my wallet. Make sure you and the gemelos eat well."

Efrén nodded as Apá buttoned his white uniform shirt. "¿Cómo sigues?"

As much as Efrén wanted to come clean and tell the truth, to open up about how tired he was, about how the worrying was getting to him, about how stressed he was at school, he knew Apá's worries were greater.

"Bien, Apá. I'm doing fine."

"Good." Apá leaned over and kissed his forehead. "Oye, estoy muy orgulloso de ti."

Efrén couldn't help but smile. "I'm proud of you too."

And with that, Apá left again for the night.

The entire apartment went silent. Efrén slipped underneath the sheets on the spot where Amá usually slept.

He took a wavering breath and looked up at the ceiling. The textured line dividing the continent had now spread across the entire living room area. All he could do was shut his eyes and pretend it wasn't there.

~~~~~~~

The next morning, a loud clang woke Efrén. The noise came from the kitchen. Efrén pushed himself up on the mattress. "Maxie, what are you doing?"

"Getting a spoon."

"Why?" He got up and scooped Max off the counter.

Max pointed to the open freezer. "For the ice cream."

"No," he said, putting him down. "You need to have breakfast first. You know that."

"I am. Ice cream!"

Efrén gave him a look. "No. Now go get dressed."

By the time Efrén placed the ice cream container back into the freezer and turned around, Max was missing. Mía stood in the living room, wiping the boogers from her eyes.

"Mía, where's Maxie?" Efrén asked.

Mía slipped her T-shirt over her head. "Hiding."

"Do you know where?"

She shook her head under the shirt.

With so few places to hide, Efrén headed straight for the bathroom. But all he found were a few forgotten books in there. No Max. He returned to the living room, panning the space for any odd bulges. Again, no luck.

He glanced over at the front door and window and—

after seeing that they were both still shut—he stepped into the kitchen and began opening the lower cabinet drawers.

"Surprise!" Max shouted, leaping out as Efrén opened the doors beneath the kitchen sink.

"Yep, you got me. Now please, won't you—" Efrén noticed Max's back and underwear dripping. "Wait, did you pee?"

Insulted, Max gave him the stink eye.

With a strange smell now reaching him, Efrén followed the water trail under the sink. "Maxie, you spilled the drain cleaner!" Without wasting a second, he picked Max up and rushed him into the bathtub.

Only Max wasn't having it and went boneless on him—a go-to move of his. "Really, Maxie. Really?"

But Efrén held him up as best he could, turned on the faucet, and aimed the shower's hand sprayer directly at him.

"Stop!" Max called. "The water's cold!"

Efrén held on to him as best he could. "Sorry, but this stuff could burn you. Now stop squirming!"

Max pulled on Efrén's hair and swung his legs wildly. One of his kicks nailed Efrén in the jaw, causing him to bite his lip.

Efrén had had enough. "I'm trying to help you!" Without thinking, Efrén smacked Max hard on the butt. Something he wished he hadn't done.

Max's eyes welled up with tears. Efrén's heart welled up with regret.

"I'm sorry, Maxie. I didn't mean to hit you. But you need to understand, the stuff you spilled is dangerous."

Max didn't answer.

In fact, he didn't answer again during breakfast when Efrén offered to warm the syrup for the freshly toasted waffles he'd found deep in the back of the freezer. Even after numerous apologies, Max sat at his seat, twirling his food around the plate while Mía sat glaring and shaking her head at Efrén. Without a doubt, it was the quietest breakfast they'd ever had.

Still soaked from the bath incident, Efrén's socks sloshed with every step, which made his twenty-minute trek to school feel longer than ever. Each sopping step reminded him of what he'd done. He wished the numbness he felt on his toes could somehow spread to the rest of him.

In spite of the rough morning, he did manage to get to school on time. He noticed a crowd of kids outside his first-period class. Efrén hurried over.

David and a few others were on their tiptoes, trying unsuccessfully to peek over the DO NOT DISTURB sign plastered over the window.

"What's going on?" Efrén asked.

David shrugged. "It *sounds* like Mr. Garrett is pounding the walls with his stapler."

"Yeah," said Ana Santana, the girl with chlorine-green blond hair. "Maybe he's decorating the room. Like a normal teacher." She got on tiptoes but even with her long legs, she couldn't see a thing.

"I know," David said, lifting up his foot and offering it to Ana, "Why don't you give me a boost?"

Ana shook her head. "No way. I'm not going anywhere near your smelly feet."

David shot her a look. "For the record, these will soon be presidential feet. And for that, I won't *let* you touch them then."

Ana crumpled her nose in disgust, but David didn't care. He'd already moved on to Efrén. "How 'bout you, F-mon?" he said, offering his foot to him. "You don't mind, right?"

Efrén shrugged and was about to reach for David's leg when Ana Santana tapped him on the shoulder.

"I have a better idea," she said, waving her phone in her hand.

Efrén stepped aside and watched as Ana raised her phone over her head and pressed it against the window for a quick video. Thirty seconds later, she brought it back down and everyone gathered around her for a peek.

Efrén stood on the tips of his toes, right behind David. Sure enough, a sea of yellow poster paper now brightened the otherwise gloomy room. This definitely wasn't normal Mr. Garrett behavior.

And if that wasn't strange enough, after the bell rang, Mr. Garrett opened the door and greeted everyone walking in with a . . . high five?

Definitely not normal.

Still feeling the soppiness of his wet socks, Efrén took the last spot in line. When he came to the door, he felt no choice but to hold the palm of his hand up flat.

"Good morning, Mr. Nava," Mr. Garrett called, slapping his hand.

Efrén gathered enough courage to lift his head. "Good morning, sir."

His teacher leaned in close. "You're all right?" he asked, in a soft voice.

Efrén didn't know what had suddenly gotten into Mr. Garrett, but one thing was for sure: he regretted having told Mr. Garrett about Amá. Efrén felt embarrassed. Didn't want the pity. Not from Mr. Garrett, not from anyone. So a quick nod was all he could give.

Mr. Garrett bent down just enough to be eye level with Efrén. "Hey, I want to thank you."

Efrén looked at him, confused.

"For reminding me why I'm here." Mr. Garrett waved him in with a smile. "Come on in. I've got an important lesson for today."

As Efrén took a seat, Mr. Garrett picked up a pile of papers from his desk and handed them to David, who never turned down a chance to leave his seat, even if it was only to simply pass out papers.

"Here are your permission slips," said Mr. Garrett from the center of the room. "I'm excited to announce that our history department has received approval for a visit to the Museum of Tolerance in LA. Of course, we will be needing some parent chaperones to join us. Please ask your parents if they'll be able to attend."

Efrén looked at the permission slip. The trip was in two weeks. Plenty of time for Amá to make it back.

"We've got a lot of material to cover before the trip."

Mr. Garrett rolled his shirt sleeves up to his elbow. There was a glimmer in his eyes that Efrén hadn't seen before. He seemed . . . excited. Efrén looked around the much-improved room, admiring the difference the new bulletin boards made. Even Mr. Garrett's desk area had gotten a makeover. His entire corner area was now plastered with certificates and college diplomas. And above them stood—not one, but two—District Teacher of the Year awards.

It was the Mr. Garrett Efrén had hoped to see.

"Now, I have to warn you," Mr. Garrett added, "during our next unit, we will be seeing some very graphic images, witnessing cruelty at its worst. However, I'd like our focus to be on the kindness, the selfless acts of bravery that took place during these trying times."

Mr. Garrett paced back and forth the same spot at the front of room. "We will be reading and hearing true audio accounts of people who risked their own lives to help complete strangers. Humanity at its finest."

Efrén thought about everything he'd shared with Mr. Garrett. *Could Mr. Garrett be doing this for me?*

Mr. Garrett clicked on his remote and started a slideshow on the projector. "If we as a society can't learn from history, sadly, we are doomed to repeat it. Now, please turn your attention to the slide in front of you. It's a poem from a German Lutheran pastor, Martin Niemöller. Anyone care to read it?"

Without skipping a beat, Jennifer Huerta put her hand up first. And of course, all the kids snickered and rolled their eyes. But Jennifer didn't seem to worry about them.

Efrén thought about how brave she was as he twirled his pencil around each of his fingers, wondering why he didn't have the courage to do the same.

Seeing no other raised hands, Mr. Garrett turned to Jennifer. "Yes, Ms. Huerta. Proceed."

Jennifer pushed her glasses up and paused to catch a breath before reading aloud.

> *"First they came for the socialists,*
> *and I did not speak out—*
> *Because I was not a socialist.*
> *Then they came for the trade unionists,*
> *and I did not speak out—*
> *Because I was not a trade unionist.*
> *Then they came for the Jews,*
> *and I did not speak out—*
> *Because I was not a Jew.*

*Then they came for me—and there*
*was no one left to speak for me."*

"Well done, Ms. Huerta. Can anyone tell me what they think it means?"

Again, her hand went up first.

"Anyone else?" asked Mr. Garrett without glancing in her direction. "Anyone else care to answer?"

Efrén wanted to raise his hand, he really did. But with his perfect attendance, straight A's, and high reading scores, he was on the brink of being labeled a nerd himself.

Calmly, Mr. Garrett paced back and forth the front of the room, searching for someone to call on. Almost immediately, his eyes locked onto David, who had *his* attention on a sketchbook.

"How about you, David?"

David did his best to hide the sketchbook under his desk, but Mr. Garrett wasn't having it. "Working on your sketches again? Hope you get my good side for a change."

The kids around David did their best to hold in their laughter.

Efrén's hand sprang up in the air, waving back and forth like the inflatable tube man at the used-car dealership across from the school. But his attempt to help his best friend went nowhere.

Mr. Garrett held out his hand, leaving David with no choice but to give up the sketchbook.

Mr. Garrett rummaged through the pages. "Ah, campaign slogans. That's what you were working on."

David didn't blush easily, but that's exactly what happened. "I'm sorry. I had an idea for a campaign poster and didn't want to forget it."

Mr. Garrett's lower lip curled upward, eventually forming a smile. "I get it. It's called being focused. That's not a bad thing, but if you're going to be ASB President, you might try to learn from people of the past to help the people of today."

Mr. Garrett's eyes searched the room. "Does anyone have any thoughts on this poem?"

Efrén raised his hand midway. As much as he wanted to share his thoughts, he might be showing up his best friend. No, he better let Jennifer take this one.

"Yes, Ms. Huerta. You are running for ASB President too, right?"

She nodded with a smile, ignoring a handful of groans in the room. "Yes, I am. David and I are the only two candidates. So one of us has to win."

"That's exciting. I'm curious to hear your thoughts."

Jennifer propped herself forward. "It's a poem, so I guess it can mean lots of things. But to me, it's about bad things happening to people and not doing anything about it. It's why I'm running for ASB President. I know I'm just a kid and can't control what's happening in the world, but I can have a say in what happens here at school . . . if you guys give me a chance."

Efrén peeked over at David sinking low into his seat.

Mr. Garret clicked his remote, pointing to a new slide. "To quote Gandhi: 'We but mirror the world. All the tendencies present in the outer world are to be found in the world of our body. If we could change ourselves, the tendencies in the world would also change.'"

He searched the room. "Anyone want to tackle this one?"

Efrén couldn't keep his hand down.

"Yes, Mr. Nava."

"What I think it means is that if you, or me, lead by example, then people around us would do the same."

"Thanks, that's exactly right. To paraphrase Gandhi, 'Be the change you want to see.'" Efrén snuck a look at David, who was still slumped in his seat.

Was he *really* the change the school needed?

# NINE

Even after the bell, David stayed slumped down in his seat, looking as if the air had somehow been squeezed out from his body. Everyone else, except for Efrén, had hurried out—including Mr. Garrett, who'd excused himself for a quick bathroom break.

Efrén walked over and patted David on the shoulder. "Hey, you all right?"

David sighed, letting out a deep breath. "Yeah. I guess. I just wasn't expecting to be put on the spot like that." He ran his fingers through his hair. "Jennifer really killed it. Sounded like a real pro."

"She is pretty smart. Super hardworking too."

David gave Efrén a look.

Efrén answered with a shrug. "What? I'm just telling it like it is."

David's head plopped against his desk. "Man, I didn't know elections were this much work. Maybe Mr. Garrett's right. I might not be cut out for this sort of thing."

"Mr. Garrett never said that."

"Didn't have to. It's pretty obvious who *he's* rooting for."

There was no arguing that point. "Maybe. But that's only because he doesn't know you like I do. That's why I think we need to rebrand you. Show the entire school how presidential you can be."

David's body sprang back up. So did his smile. "You're right! I can't just count on my popularity. I've got to focus on the issues and keep the campaign clean . . . like a baby's butt."

Efrén crunched his forehead. "I'm not so sure baby butts are all that clean."

"Of course they are. Otherwise they'd get all rashy." Now reenergized, David flung his backpack over his shoulder and gestured toward the door. "Come on. We've got an election to win! Ms. Salas says we need a short presentation for next week's morning announcements. I'm thinking of filming a campaign video. You can be in it too, if you want."

Efrén took a deep breath, bracing himself for one of David's crazy plans.

"Our video needs to be funny, but deep," David said. "Without sundering my opponent."

"I think you mean slandering. Like politicians do on TV ads," Efrén said, walking toward the door.

"Yeah, none of that."

*None of that?* It was music to Efrén's ears. Was David finally taking things more seriously? Had Efrén been wrong? Maybe there was nothing to actually worry about.

"When I win," David added, jamming his thumb into his chest, "I want to know it was because the best man won. That's why my presentation's gonna be a music video. And not just any video," he said, "a rap video!"

Efrén squeegeed his face with the palm of his hand. Immediately, his mind replayed part of his talk with Jennifer. Especially the part when she hugged him. Had the election been that day, Efrén just might've voted for her instead. And this was not okay with Efrén.

*No! No colluding with the enemy.* He had to stay loyal to David at all costs.

Maybe David just needed a little help, a little motivation to act more like . . . well, like Jennifer.

"As your campaign manager," Efrén said, "it's my job to advise you, tell you things you might not want to hear. Things like, I'm not sure this rap video's a good idea."

David stopped under the classroom doorway with a blank stare. "Good point. Anyone can make a rap video. See, that's why I pay you the big bucks." He raised a hand up high in the air, setting up for a high five. "So I'm gonna freestyle."

Efrén lifted his arm and—with a forced smile—slapped David's hand. He may have been smiling on the outside, but he was definitely wincing inside.

David reached for the door and shut it behind him before breaking out into a rhyme down the hall.

*"Hold up, take a listen*
*I'm running for ASB President, and yes, I glisten*
*I will make it happen, I have a plan.*
*For a better school, I am your man.*
*Everyone knows I am the GOAT,*
*so get out today, get out and vote."*

Efrén's mind struggled for just the right thing to say. "I can't picture anybody doing what you just did."

David's smile was wily. "I know, right?"

David's extra bounce lasted all day. It even made him pedal extra hard while giving Efrén a ride home on the handlebars of his bike. David made it a point to sway around the many potholes on the road, but occasionally stood up and leaned forward for an added burst of speed. This made the road feel bumpier, but Efrén didn't mind. Knowing he'd make it on time to pick up the twins made the pain worth it.

David greeted anyone and everyone they passed—even the shirtless old guy who liked to read the newspaper from his porch while rubbing his hairy belly.

Efrén gripped the handlebar cushion and clung on tight for dear life, all while trying to act as cool as possible.

"Are you sure your grandma won't mind having the little traviesos over?"

"You kidding? She loves babying people. Especially pint-size twins with adorable cheeks. I'm telling you, the trick's gonna be getting them back from her. Even with her arthritis, we might have to pry them from her hands."

Efrén shook his head and cringed. "I don't know what's worse: your jokes or these potholes."

"Ha, ha," David said, purposely hitting a dip on the road.

Good thing for Efrén's butt that Pío Pico Elementary was just around the corner. When they got to the school, the sidewalk was filled with moms pushing fancy secondhand strollers, chatting, exchanging the latest neighborhood chisme.

Efrén tried keeping his head down. The neighborhood was full of chismosos and the last thing he wanted was anyone talking about him. Or Amá.

Fortunately, the foot traffic didn't slow David in the least. In fact, it just seemed to encourage him to speed up. "Hold on, F-mon."

"What do you think I'm doing?"

Except for one close call, el Periquito Blanco stood up on his bike and successfully zigzagged his way around everyone, finally reaching the playground. "See, told you we'd make it before the bell."

Efrén leaped off the bike, pulling the wedgie out

of his butt. "I'm thinking about taking the bus next time."

David leaned his bike beside the outdoor lunch tables. "It's not about the ride. It's the company that matters."

"I don't know. Tons of really nice old people ride the bus." Efrén took a seat beside David. "It's weird coming back here, huh?"

"Dude. I still have nightmares about this place."

Efrén laughed, and then pointed to a dirt patch separating the lunch and play area. "You remember the marble game? When we played Rigoberto and Rodrigo, and pretended like we didn't know how to play?"

"Hey, they're the ones who insisted on playing for keeps. They were trying to con *us*."

"I can't believe we won so many marbles. Remember when the bell rang and your shorts fell down as you started running to the line?"

"Yep, the weight from the marbles made my shorts drop down to my ankles. I tripped and all the marbles came flying out of my pockets." David snort-laughed. "Man, we caused such a mess. Every kid out in recess came running over. It was a total marble free-for-all."

Efrén leaned back, laughing. "There was so much screaming the teachers came out from the lounge, trying to figure out what was going on."

"That was embarrassing." David shook his head, sighing deeply. "That's the same day I switched over to boxer shorts. You know, just in case."

"It doesn't matter if everyone laughed. You were little."

"You didn't laugh. In fact, you never do."

With bleary eyes, David held out his hand. Efrén couldn't believe he'd ever considered voting for Jennifer. He extended his hand and the two dapped in perfect sync, with Efrén easing up at the end, letting David get the thumb war pin. No matter how much Efrén respected Jennifer, there was no way he was going to betray David. NO WAY! Now, if only he could tell him about what was going on with Amá.

The walk to David's house went smoothly, especially now that Max and Mía were once again talking to Efrén. They couldn't wait to meet David's grandma, especially after he told them that she always kept a freezer full of ice cream. Which was true. The only thing not true was the reason for the visit. Efrén told David Amá had changed her work hours.

David's house was small and simple, but it had a big yard. Actually, it had an enormous yard. It had to be, considering the size of the huge oak tree that towered in it. This broccoli-shaped giant was the most amazing tree Efrén had ever seen in person.

Efrén and David often talked about building a tree house right smack in the middle. David wanted to have both Wi-Fi and a microwave so they could stream movies and eat popcorn. He also insisted that it have no ladder, just a climbing rope designed to keep all wimps out—especially girls.

David even drew up blueprints and posted them over his bed, waiting for his dad's help to make it happen. But that was just an empty promise, like the one he'd made about visiting often.

In the meantime, the tree was pretty fun as it was. So was the knee-high grass that allowed them to hide during their infamous walnut battles with the other kids on the block. Games there might've been painful, but they were equally fun.

"Max. Mía. You guys better be on your best behavior.

David's grandma is going to be watching you, but she's got a bad hip and can't chase after you. Okay?"

Both Max and Mía hooked pinkies and promised.

David reached into his pocket and pulled out a tiny soccer keychain with the LA Galaxy team logo just about smeared off it. The second he opened the front door, his little kitten, Oreo, came running over.

Max's eyes sprang wide open. "¡Un gatito!" he said, barging forward with both arms extended in front of him. Fortunately for Oreo, Efrén managed to pull him back by the shirt.

"No, you don't. You're going to scare her." Efrén bent down until he was eye level with Max. "You wouldn't want to scare the kitten, would you?"

Max shook his head. "Don't worry, gatitos love me!"

David scooped up the squealing kitten and cuddled her in the fold of his arm. "She likes it when you scratch her."

Efrén took a step back. "Not me. I'm allergic, remember?"

Max and Mía began raking their fingers along her back, making Oreo purr.

Just then, David's grandma came into the living

room. Her cane didn't seem to slow her down much. "These two precious little ones must be Max and Mía."

"Hello, Ms. Deegen," Efrén said. "Thank you so much for agreeing to watch them while David and I work on the campaign."

She smiled. "Hi, Efrén." But it was obvious that her attention was already on the twins. She came up to Max first and squeezed his chubby cheeks like most people did who met him for the first time.

Max didn't mind. His cheeks were used to getting pinched. Mía, not so much. She immediately covered her cheeks with her hands, making Ms. Deegen laugh.

"You two"—she turned to David—"go work on that project. I'll watch these adorable children."

David gave her a peck on the cheek, and then lowered Oreo onto the floor. "Thank you, Grandma!"

With that, the boys headed to David's room.

The hallway walls were almost completely covered with picture frames, mostly of David back when he was little, back before his parents separated—back before his mother began to drink a lot and David's grandma had to take him in.

Efrén pointed at a photo of David being bathed in

the kitchen sink. "Man, you were chubbier than Max. Look at those arms."

David laughed. "I know, right? I keep telling Grandma that must be some other adorable-looking kid." He reached for the door to his room, sprouting a huge grin. "Wait 'til you see my new toy."

*New toy?* Knowing David, a new toy could be anything. A new slingshot, a new skateboard, maybe even new jewelry.

"Let me guess, you got a new—" Efrén's jaw dropped as he entered the room. In the corner on David's desk sat a new iPhone.

Efrén rushed to pick it up, his entire face gleaming. "Oh, my God. When did you get this?"

"Yesterday. My mom sent it to me. Said this way we could FaceTime with each other anytime we want. Maybe my dad will get one too." David's eyes welled up just a bit. "But I was thinking we could use it to film the campaign video. I've got the perfect thing to wear too."

He rushed over to his closet and pulled out a white dress shirt and a tie. "Grandma bought me this for"— he paused, embarrassed—"for Sunday school. She says it'll keep me from getting possessed like mom."

"How is she doing?" Efrén asked.

"Better," David said, slipping into the dress shirt and snapping on the clip-on tie. "She just got a new job and is taking classes at a community college. I think she'll make it this time."

This wasn't the first time Efrén had heard David talk like this. He liked seeing David happy and filled with hope but hated seeing him hurt each time his mom relapsed and started drinking again. Nevertheless, he smiled and nodded. "Of course, she will."

David took a deep breath before he reached for his phone, entered his password, and handed it back to Efrén. "Where should we film?"

Efrén looked around the room, only now noticing how tidy everything was. "You even cleaned your room! Last time I was here, I accidently sat on a pile of dirty socks and underwear."

"That's not true," David said, grinning. "The socks weren't dirty."

"Nasty," Efrén said. He held up the phone and pointed at the desk. "I think this desk makes you look presidential. What do you think?"

"Indubitably," said David. "See, the clothes are making me sound smarter too."

Efrén focused the camera directly at him. "All right, Mr. Smarty-pants—I mean Smarty-shirt—why don't you tell us about your presidential platform?"

"My what?"

"Why don't you tell us about all the amazing things you are planning to do as president."

David looked up at the ceiling, "I don't know . . . how about getting rid of homework?"

"Um!" Efrén put the camera down. "You know you can't really do that, right?"

"I don't know," David said, shifting his butt at the edge of his chair. "What does a president even do?"

Efrén shook his head. "Maybe you should have paid less attention to the conchas Ms. Salas bought and more attention to the ASB candidate meeting."

David glared at Efrén, and then down at the ground. "It's not that big a deal. I'll put together the biggest school party ever and everyone will be happy. Besides, if I win, I'll have Jennifer as vice president. You know she's gonna be full of suggestions. I can just follow her lead."

Efrén sighed. "Dude, then why are we voting for you?" Immediately Efrén regretted his words.

But it was too late. The room felt suddenly hotter.

"You don't think I can do this, do you?"

"No, it's not like that."

David's nostrils flared. "This whole neighborhood thinks I'm just some goofy gringo to laugh at." David's voice began to break. "Being president is my chance to prove everyone wrong."

Efrén's mind raced for a response.

"I guess the joke's on me, huh?" David continued. "Actually," he said, correcting himself, "I *am* the joke. Mr. Garrett made that perfectly clear in class."

"You're not a joke, David."

"Oh, please," David scoffed. "El Periquito Blanco . . . that's what kids call me. They don't even bother to do it behind my back. They think I'm too stupid to understand them making fun of my white skin and big nose."

"It's just a joke. They're just messing with you. No big deal."

David shook his head, like there was nothing more to say.

Efrén wanted to fix this. Wanted to tell him all about Jennifer. About her parents being undocumented. About her wanting to make a real difference at school. But that was a secret. He couldn't repeat that.

He thought again about why he hadn't told David

about Amá having been deported. They'd known each other for so many years. Shared so much—like countless Jarritos sodas.

Telling David about Amá would make a huge difference. He'd have to understand.

*My Amá got deported.* Four simple words. That was it. And yet, the words carried so much hurt they seemed to swell and get lodged in his throat.

Efrén drew a deep breath. Finally, he spoke—only something totally different came out. "I'd better go. Maxie and Mía must be driving your grandmother crazy." He gently tossed David's phone onto the bed.

"Fine," answered David. "Don't worry about the video. I can do it myself."

"I know you can." Efrén left the door open just in case David called him back. But he never did.

That night, after eventually getting the twins to bed, Efrén headed back to the bathtub, this time, with pillow and blanket in tow.

He opened the library copy of *The House on Mango Street*, turned to the page where he'd left off, and tried reading. But his mind shifted to David. He never meant to hurt his friend's feelings.

It wasn't that Efrén didn't trust him with the family's secret. Actually, it was the exact opposite. Efrén knew David would go home and tell his grandma. He knew they'd bring over cooked meals and probably offer him some money. That was the problem!

David knew just about everything about Efrén. Knew about his family living in a tiny studio apartment. Knew about their sleeping on mattresses on the floor. Knew about Efrén's secondhand clothes and toys. And yet, David had never pitied him. Efrén wanted to keep it that way.

Efrén stared at the drip coming from the faucet and thought about the old story he'd heard about a Dutch boy who'd saved a village by plugging a hole in the dam with his thumb. Eventually, he pulled off his sock with his other foot and stuck his big toe inside the faucet.

He might not be a hero like that boy, but he could at least try to make things right between him and David. He had to.

First Amá, now this. Efrén closed his book and blessed himself with the sign of the cross. "Diosito, it's me. I know that you've been busy looking out for Amá and helping us to get her back. But if you can, could you help me patch things up with David too? He's my best friend. And I kind of need one right now. Gracias."

Efrén leaned back against his pillow. His eyelids became unbearably heavy, and even with the bright lights shining above, he couldn't fight off the sleep.

# TEN

Efrén felt a gentle nudge on his shoulder.

"Mijo. Mijo," said Apá. "I'm sorry, but I need to take a quick shower." He pointed to the dark circle on his armpit. "Can't go to work all apestoso."

Efrén stretched out his arms, remembering he was still in the bathtub. "Oh, hey, Apá. Sorry, I fell asleep reading."

Apá laughed to himself. "I figured." He bent down and wrapped his arms around Efrén. "Here, let me give you a hand." Apá scooped Efrén out with little effort.

Apá's strength surprised Efrén. "I can't believe you can still do that."

"Actually, I'm pretty surprised too," said Apá, again laughing. "Someday, you will be too big for me to do that. But today is not that day. So come on, you need to get to bed. It's too early for you to be up."

"Okay, Apá." Efrén tucked the library book under his arm, carefully bear-hugged his blanket and pillow, and headed to the living room area. Max was spread across the mattress, snoring just slightly, while Mía clung to her naked plush doll.

Rays of blue moonlight poked through the broken blinds. Efrén looked over at the empty mattress and shook his head. The sheets were still folded just like the night before. Efrén didn't understand where Apá found the energy. Even after all the overtime trying to raise money to bring back Amá, he still found time to worry about them.

This was all he needed to see. *If Apá can be this strong, why can't I?* Efrén wanted to solve *his* problems too. It was then that he decided to tell David everything. He still didn't know what he was going to say. Or where to start for that matter. But he knew the words would come when the moment was right.

They had to. Their friendship was at stake.

Efrén wanted to get to his own school with enough time to find David, so he dropped off Max and Mía a little earlier than normal. The three of them arrived so early that they were first in the school breakfast line. Max had his heart set on some pan dulce and chocolate milk, Mía on silver dollar pancakes—the ones with maple syrup bits inside—that the school sometimes served. Sadly, both had to settle for generic brand Cheerios and slightly bruised bananas.

With the twins fed and the playground supervisor now watching over them, Efrén hurried to get to his school.

The entire main school entrance was empty this early. Most kids hung out in the cafeteria area, eating breakfast. Something he'd never done before. Not with Amá's breakfast milagros taking place every morning. Check that. With the milagros Amá *used* to make.

Efrén walked over to the tables, wondering if his school was serving the same cereal breakfast as Max and Mía's. He took a quick look at what the kids around him had on their plates. Nope. *His* school was serving the tiny pancakes Mía had wanted.

He was about to get in line when a tap on his shoulder startled him. It was Abraham, the school's very own chisme machine. Whether the gossip was true or not, he was always in the middle of it. "Dude, David won!"

"What are you talking about? No one's voted yet."

Abraham laughed. "No one has to. Jennifer dropped out of the race. Which means that David wins." This time, he raised up his hand for a high five.

Efrén's mouth went wide open and froze. His mind couldn't accept the news, even as he slapped hands with Abraham. "Wait, there's no way Jennifer would just quit like that."

Abraham shook his head. "She didn't just drop out of the election. She dropped out of school."

"What? Why?"

"Who cares?" said Abraham, shrugging. "David's gonna be our president. He said the first thing he would do is make sure the school starts serving Takis for breakfast—nitro flavored! Man, I can't wait."

Efrén's stomach tightened. And the idea of eating Takis for breakfast had nothing to do with it. He needed to get to the bottom of this now.

He bolted up the stairway leading to the library, skipping multiple steps at a time. Winded, he entered through the double doors, hoping to find the one person who could give him the answers he needed—Jennifer's friend, Han Pham.

Han was seated near the back of the library, by the reference section. The book in front of her was closed and she had both hands over her face.

"Hey, Han. Are you all right?"

She lowered her hands and looked directly at Efrén. Something was wrong. Her eyes were glassy and tinted pink. Obviously, she'd been crying.

"What's wrong?" asked Efrén.

She didn't answer. She just looked down at her closed book.

"Look," said Efrén. "I know that we were on opposite sides of this election, but Jennifer is my friend too. I know she really wanted to win. Why would she just quit like this? And why are people saying she dropped out of school?"

Han's upper lip curled. Something he said had rubbed Han the wrong way. "For your information, she didn't just quit. ICE did a raid." Her faced squished together as she did her best not to cry.

Efrén's stomach sank. "Oh, my God. Was she"—he could barely say the word—"deported?"

Han's shook her head as she sobbed. Yet somehow, she found the strength to continue speaking. "There was a sweep at the Northgate Market on First and Harbor. My neighbor Diego Flores saw the whole thing. Said that men in black vests and assault rifles burst inside and cornered the adults, including her mom. He said that her mom screamed for Jennifer to run home. But Jennifer wouldn't leave her side. She even dropped to her knees and tried pleading with the men."

"Oh, my God. Is Jennifer okay? Where is she? I thought she was born in the US."

"She had to go to Mexico, with her mom . . . or social services was going to take her." Han buried her face on the fold of her elbow. "I didn't even get to say good-bye to her."

Efrén's stomach twisted and churned in every direction. "Poor Jennifer," he said. He couldn't believe what was happening. He knew things like this happened every day, but not to people he knew, people he cared for.

Efrén cleared his throat. "Is there anything we can do for her?"

"I've been thinking about that." Han wiped her nose with a tissue. "She wanted to use the ASB position to bring more attention to this problem. She wanted to start a campaign to raise awareness, maybe start a support group to help families. But now she can't do anything. Part of me thinks that I should run in her place, keep fighting in her place."

"You can do that?"

"Sure. Anyone who attended the meeting can run. But can you picture me trying to speak in front of the entire school? No way."

Han sniffled and wiped away her tears. "She had this Spanish line that she used to say a lot."

"¿Somos semillitas?" Efrén said, beating her to the words.

"Yeah, that's it. How did you know that?"

Efrén's face grew blank. "She told me." He gave a hard swallow. *Nos quisieron enterrar, pero no sabían que éramos semillas.* "It's a Mexican saying. 'They tried to bury us . . . but they didn't know we were seeds.' Jennifer told me her mom used to say it to her all the time."

The words were as clear as day. So clear, they stayed in Efrén's mind for the rest of the morning.

When his first period class started, Efrén took his seat but mostly just stared at the whiteboard in front of him. He tuned out the kids around him, including everything Mr. Garrett said.

He trusted Apá. Knew he'd never give up on getting Amá back. *But what if he couldn't? What if this problem was too big even for him to fix?* The thought sent a shiver down Efrén's spine.

When class ended, he calmly made his way to his next classroom and waited outside. Each period went more or less the same way. Except for math, when Efrén opened a new browser tab in his Chromebook and did a search: DETAINING CENTER FOR KIDS. What he found shook him. He scrolled down page after page of photos showing little children behind chain-link fences, sleeping on tiled floors, aluminum benches, and—in some cases—each other's arms.

He thought back to what Jennifer had said and did a search for CHICKEN FARMS. A few of the images were alike. Many, though, showed chickens running freely in open yards.

Efrén slammed the Chromebook shut. He could feel his chest heaving and knew it was simply a matter of seconds before he'd begin crying.

He reached for a bathroom pass and held it up for Ms. Covey to see. She nodded and gave him a thumbs-up. Efrén hurried to the boys' restroom and locked himself in the last stall. He sat on the toilet and pressed his fist hard against his forehead.

It wasn't fair. If the roles were flipped and he'd been

the one deported, Jennifer would be taking a stand and fighting for him. He couldn't sit around and do nothing.

Jennifer deserved to be there. She also deserved to be ASB President. Not David.

As much as he tried to forget about the idea, the more it seemed to take root in his brain.

The rest of the school day, Efrén managed to avoid David, even ate lunch alone by the stairwell. And when the final bell rang, he hurried and made a quick stop at Ms. Salas's room before going to pick up Max and Mía.

After school, Efrén gathered up all the dirty laundry. Worried about using up the last of his money, he searched every kitchen drawer, gathering up all the loose change he could find. Then he loaded up a rusty Radio Flyer wagon with a trash bag full of clothes, a carton of generic laundry soap, and—of course—Max and Mía.

Once at the laundromat, Efrén separated the family's clothes into two carts. One for colors, one for whites, while Max and Mía watched an episode of *Dora the Explorer* in the kids' area.

That's when David rode up to the doorway. He parked his bike against the glass door.

"Hey, F-mon! I've been looking everywhere for you. Hey, no worries about what happened yesterday. It's over. I did it. I won!" He held up his fist for a dap.

Efrén half-heartedly returned the fist bump.

"Dude, you're not still mad. Are you?" David asked.

"Nah, just got a lot on my plate."

David surveyed the two piles of clothes. "I can see that." Without missing a beat, he reached over and picked up a tiny pair of Superman briefs. "Are these yours?" he asked, holding up the underwear for everyone in the room to see.

"No. Those are Maxie's. And FYI . . . they're still kind of wet."

"Gross." David flicked the undies back onto the pile and wiped his hand on the side of his Lakers jersey.

"Oh, I almost forgot." David pulled out his iPhone. "Check this out. Han sent me this message. It's for you. From Jennifer. It's in Spanish."

Efrén took the phone and scrolled down the screen. It was a photo of a drawing done on lined paper, a small plant blooming out from a pile of dirt. The words *ERES UNA SEMILLA* followed underneath.

Efrén shut his eyes.

"Dude, what's wrong? Does it say something bad?"

"No," Efrén said, opening his eyes and handing back the phone. "It's just something she once told me." Only it was more than that. Efrén ran his fingers through his hair and let out a big sigh. "Dude, there's something I really gotta tell you."

"All righty." David took a seat on a washer. "What's up?"

"I know this position isn't going to change the world. But I've got to do something." Efrén fidgeted with one of Maxie's tube socks. "My parents gave up everything for me. I need to do something for them. Jennifer taught me that."

David scrunched his forehead. "What are you talking about?"

Efrén took a big gulp of air. "I stopped by Ms. Salas's office. Told her I'm running for ASB President too. She okayed it."

"You mean vice president, don't you?"

Efrén looked away.

"You're kidding, right?" Efrén gazed down at the scratched tile floor, trying desperately not to make eye contact with David. But the hurt wasn't just on David's face. It was in his voice too. "Why would you do that?"

"It's not for me. David, you know you're my best friend, and I'd never do something to hurt you. But I need to do this. Please try to understand."

"What's there to understand? You're stabbing me in the back."

"No, it's not like that."

"Yes, it is. It's exactly like that. I mean, look at you. You have absolutely everything. You're great at school. Good at sports. Your mom and dad . . . they worship you. I've seen the way they look at you. My dad won't even visit me. Just sends me money." David's voice shook. "Being president is my chance to prove everyone wrong. But that's okay. I mean, you have to have everything, don't you?"

*What about Amá? Do I have her?* Efrén's thoughts shouted back. "It's not something you'd understand."

"Oh, so now I'm too dumb to understand? You know what?"—David leaned in and got in Efrén's face—"I don't need you on my side to win the election. In fact, I don't need you as a friend either."

Efrén didn't know how to answer and stood there, eyes blinking.

With that, David stormed out of the laundromat,

hopped back onto his bike, and pedaled away. Too late, Efrén ran after his friend.

"David! Wait!" Efrén hollered from the sidewalk. But David never looked back.

Amá was never very big on watching TV, not even the telenovelas that all the other mothers on the block raved about. So Efrén felt bad about plopping the twins in front of the set and letting Elmo babysit. But he didn't have the strength to deal with Max's high energy or Mía's need to cuddle. *Besides*, Efrén told himself, *PBS shows are educational*.

He sat at the kitchen table with his head plopped down, letting the cool surface soothe his aching head. *What a mess!* Amá was gone. Apá was killing himself to raise the money to get her back. Jennifer was gone. And now, Efrén's friendship with David was over.

Out of the blue, Efrén heard the hint of a whistle. He looked up. At first, he thought it came from the TV, but the screen just showed Mr. Noodle, pretending to play an ear of corn as if it were a trumpet.

Then he heard a whistle again, only much clearer now. Max's and Mía's heads perked up in perfect unison, and they turned to each other. "Apá!" they both hollered. There was no mistaking Apá's special entrance melody.

Before Efrén could react, the twins were already out the door and running down the stairs. *Why was Apá whistling? He only did that whenever he had . . . GOOD NEWS!*

Efrén rushed outside and down the stairway only to find Max and Mía latched onto each of Apá's legs like little koalas on a eucalyptus branch.

Apá looked up at Efrén, smiling. Somehow, Apá was full of energy again.

Efrén couldn't wait to hear the news. "What happened?"

Apá laughed as he strained to climb the stairway. "I joined a cundina at work." He held up a tiny slip of paper with the number one on it.

"A what?"

"It's a group fund where everyone puts money in and then take turns borrowing the money each week but—¡No importa! I GOT THE MONEY!"

Efrén rushed to Apá and wrapped him up with a huge hug.

Now without the need of overtime, Apá took everyone to the playground and the four of them spent the next hour playing a game of tag. As Efrén took a break to get water, he looked back and watched Apá chase Mía up the spiral slide.

The moment was almost perfect.

Soon, Amá would be coming home where she belonged, and then the family would be whole again.

Despite feeling bad about David, the idea of having Amá back gave Efrén an extra spring in his step this Friday morning. Once she was back, he'd finally find the courage to tell David the truth and patch things up with him. Until then, he needed to focus on helping Apá with everything at home and preparing for the election.

To make sure he wouldn't be late to school anymore, he broke one of Amá's rules and took the twins to school on his bicycle, with Max sitting sidesaddle over the main crossbar and Mía across the foam-covered handlebars. It took a bit of getting used to the added weight—and Max's wiggling—but eventually Efrén managed. And riding to school also gave him plenty of time to visit the ASB student center and get started on a few campaign posters.

As he locked up his bicycle, his mind scrolled through a long list of possible campaign slogans:

*Efrén Nava, Someone You Can Trust.* Nope, not after what he'd done to David.

*¡Efrén Nava para Presidente!* Nope.

*Efrén Nava: Make School Great Again!* Definitely not!

*Efrén Nava for ASB President.* "Efrén Nava for ASB President." He liked the sound of that.

He darted up to the main stairway to Ms. Salas's ASB room. She always kept her door wide open. It wasn't unusual for students—some she didn't even know—to randomly stop by and reach into the cookie jar she kept by the door.

"Good morning, Ms. Salas."

"Oh, hi, Efrén. Here to work on your campaign posters?"

"Yes, ma'am. And thank you again for allowing me to run, especially on such late notice."

"Well, you did attend the meeting and you do meet all the academic requirements."

"I'm behind, but I've got some ideas for slogans. Hopefully, they'll work well enough to get me elected."

Efrén eyed the cookie jar. "Mind if I take a cookie?"

"Not at all. That's why I bake them," she said, adjusting her glasses. "You might want to take one to your friend."

"Friend?"

Ms. Salas nodded. "Yes, David. He's in the workroom, designing posters. I think it's great that you two can compete against each other and still be friends."

"Yeah, it is." With that, Efrén slipped a cookie into his pocket and headed for the workroom. Sure enough, David sat on a stool alone, his forehead scrunched and his tongue hanging out to the side.

"Oh, hey," Efrén said, plopping the cookie beside David.

David looked up. "Hey."

Efrén picked up a bright green sheet of poster paper and took a seat at a table containing just about every kind of art tool imaginable. He reached for a thick marker while studying the sample fonts on the wall posters.

There were so many styles he could copy; unfortunately, all the cool ones were way too complicated for him to even try. He picked up a pencil instead and decided to try his best cursive. But the letters came out uneven and curved in different directions.

His eyes wandered to David's posters. *His* artwork was amazing. Each of his letters had a shadowy effect that made them pop out as if they were 3D. It must have taken him forever to make.

Efrén couldn't remember ever seeing his friend— former friend?—so focused on anything before. Being president really did mean a lot to David. Maybe Efrén was wrong. Maybe running against him was a mistake.

Looking down at his own work, Efrén realized how difficult this campaign would be without David to help. Efrén sighed. If he were going to win, it would be the message—not the artwork—that would get him there.

After a few failed attempts at drawing his name, he considered typing out the message, then printing and gluing the letters onto the poster. But then, out of nowhere, a pack of stencils fell on top of his supplies. He looked over and watched David retake his seat as if nothing had happened.

Efrén eyed the stencils. All he had to do now was trace the cutouts and presto—perfect letters.

"Thank you," Efrén said.

But Efrén's thank-you went unanswered.

Efrén and David continued working side by side, never speaking a word, until the bell rang.

Ms. Salas sat at her desk, watching Efrén and David both stop for one more cookie before leaving for first period.

Down the hallway, the two boys made their way to class in total silence. The self-imposed silence continued well past the fifteen-minute nutrition break, when the former best friends both returned to the workroom to complete another poster.

As helpful as the stencils were, they still took a long time to use. So when lunch hour came, David and Efrén were back in the workroom. Except this time, just as David got up to leave, Efrén pushed back his stool. "David?"

David paused briefly by the doorway.

Efrén rushed over to him. "I know what I did seems messed up. But I wouldn't have done it if I didn't have a good reason."

David stopped to listen. "Fine. Go ahead and explain. What was worth stabbing me in the back over?"

There was a brief stare down. Efrén knew what he

needed to do. After all, David was his best friend and wouldn't tell a soul.

He had nothing to fear. He took a deep breath and could feel the words building up inside. Unfortunately, they weren't alone. Shame came along for the ride.

Was he embarrassed to admit that both Amá and Apá were undocumented? No. That wasn't it.

Efrén's tears welled up as the back of his throat began to feel raw. It wasn't the truth that embarrassed him. It was breaking down in front of David.

"I'm sorry, David." And with that, Efrén hurried off.

Once Efrén and the twins were home after school, he spread the supplies and poster paper that Ms. Salas had given him over the kitchen table. Max and Mía immediately took a seat next to him. "Guys, I need to make a bunch of posters."

"Can I make one?" asked Max. "I'm good at art! Huh, Mía?"

"Yeah, me too! I want to help!"

"I appreciate the—" Efrén looked at the wide-eyed faces staring up at him. He didn't want a second round of Max's silent treatment—or Mía's.

"All right, here," he said, handing each a blank sheet of poster paper. "Just make sure everything is neat and easy to read."

Neither of the twins wasted a moment. Mía went straight for a ruler and Sharpie while Max went for a brush and purple tempera paint.

Efrén looked carefully at his poster. There was definitely something missing. He bit down on his lower lip, trying to figure out what he needed to change. He reached for the packet of stencils and got to work. When he was done, he stood back and admired his handiwork. "What do you guys think?"

Mía gave it a quick scan. "Needs color."

## EFRÉN NAVA 4 ASB PRESIDENT
## "THE CHANGE YOU WANT TO SEE"

"Yep. It needs a lot more color," Max replied, not bothering to even take a look.

Efrén rubbed his chin. "I don't know. I kind of like it this way. How are you two doing with the posters?"

"Me, I'm pretty much done," said Mía, holding up her poster.

Efrén's heart swelled. With large, curvy letters, the

bright red poster read: "Vote for Efren, BEST BIG BRUTHER!"

"I'm done too. See?" chimed in Max while smearing the purple paint on his face. "I did it myself."

Efrén's heart sank as he read it:

VOT FOAR EFREN
I LUV HIM

He leaned down and squeezed the twins tightly. "These are the most amazing posters I have ever seen."

# ELEVEN

"All right, I think we've got everything we need. Mía, you got the tape?"

Mía raised her hand and twirled the blue roll around her arm like it was a tiny Hula-Hoop.

David had gotten a head start with his campaign and had signs all over the school. It was Friday night, and Efrén didn't want to wait for the following Monday to put up the posters they'd just made. No way. He decided instead to take the twins back to school with him. The trick would be to get them home before it started getting dark.

As tempting as it was, he chose to leave his bike behind. Lugging the little ones down the block to their school on his bike was one thing, but there was no way Amá would ever approve of his taking them across

Civic Center Drive.

"Maxie, can you grab my posters?"

"Sure." Max wrapped his arms around the posters and was heading toward the door when he froze in place. "Oh, wait," he said, running back over to the kitchen table. "We almost forgot ours."

Efrén tossed the black trash bag filled with posters over his back. "That's okay, guys. We can leave those two here. You know, tape them to the fridge."

The little ones gave him a look.

"So I can see them every day."

Mía held onto her scowl while Max's eyes began to well up.

Guilt booted Efrén in the gut. "What am I thinking? There's no way I can leave my two secret weapons at home. These two posters are going to get me elected."

Max's brown eyes lit up like shiny pennies while Mía's face softened into a smile.

Max didn't waste any time finding a spot for his poster. The second they set foot onto campus, he rushed down the main corridor and claimed a spot over the drinking fountain.

Mía looked up at Efrén, nodding. "He picked a good

spot. A *really* good spot." Wearing a huge smile, she took hold of the tape and bolted after him.

Efrén waited behind, looking around at the empty halls. There was something different about the place, and not just the lack of usual kid-related noise. Nope, there was something else.

Even though it had only been about two hours since school had let out, the campus was pretty much abandoned by the time they arrived. The only people visible were the handful of teachers heading out, many hauling teacher supply carts behind them—and Joe, the custodian, putting a water hose in the back of his cart.

*So this is what happens after hours.* Efrén looked down at the wet concrete below his feet. It'd only been a few hours, but already the school was prepared for the following week. It was nice—the same feeling he had when Amá was still home. He missed coming home from school and finding a warm meal and a clean apartment.

But after this weekend, things would go back to normal—he was sure of it. Apá had the money and it would bring Amá back.

"Wait up, guys," Efrén called out while running to help Max down from the top of the drinking fountain.

Max's poster was right above the most heavily used drinking fountain in the entire school. Efrén stared at it. *Everyone* would see this!

"Maxie, don't you think we should put this somewhere else—you know, so it doesn't get wet. You know how sloppy kids are when they drink water." Efrén crossed his fingers as Max tilted his head and rubbed the tip of his chin as if combing through an actual beard.

"Nope. This is good. Right, Mía?"

Mía looked up at Efrén. Then over at the poster. "Yep. This is perfect."

One thing was for sure—these posters would get people talking. And if the internet had taught Efrén anything, it was that any publicity is good publicity.

"All right, fine. But we've got a lot more posters to put up. You guys ready to move at super speed?"

Max and Mía got into their starting positions.

"Speedy Gonzales speed!" And with that, Efrén's ASB presidential campaign was underway. Max raced over to the main quad area and taped a poster to a tree while Mía centered hers onto the science lab door.

Efrén, however, chose to start at the far end of the hallway. Just as he unrolled a poster and was about to pull the roll of tape from his pocket, he caught sight of an open door. He peeked inside and did a double take. There stood Mr. Garrett, dressed in a George Washington costume.

"Mr. Garrett?"

Poor Mr. Garrett jumped out of his skin. "Geez, Efrén. You practically scared me out of my . . . wooden teeth."

"Wait, WHY are you dressed like that?"

Mr. Garrett's face turned bright red as he slipped the wig back into a bag. "Yeah, we're going to be studying the Constitution next. I thought this might help. But what are *you* doing here?"

"Putting up posters. For my campaign." Efrén entered the room. "I have some good news—about my mom."

"Is she back?"

"Not yet. But she will be soon."

Mr. Garrett nodded. "Good. Because no child should ever be separated from a parent."

"Speaking of children," Efrén said lightheartedly, "I'd better get my brother and sister. Gonna shut the door now"—Efrén did his best to hide his grin—"so you can finish trying on your costume."

Again, a flush crept across Mr. Garrett's face.

That evening, Apá picked up a bag of churros for dessert on his way home. However, the real treat was getting to talk with Amá on the phone again. Apá had asked Efrén not to ask her when she was coming back, but that didn't stop Max and Mía. In fact, they took turns telling her the same things over and over again:

"Amá, we miss you."

"Amá, when are you coming back?"

"Amá, please come home."

Efrén was happy just hearing her voice.

In a few days, she'd be back home. And there was no way Efrén was going to let things go back to normal. No way was he going to hide out in the bathroom reading while Amá cooked and cleaned for everyone. He would go online. Look up how to make pancakes or scrambled eggs, maybe even learn how to make milagros of his own.

With the sugar rush from the churros out of their system and the copy of Dr. Seuss's book *Oh, the Places You'll Go!* that Max borrowed from Ms. Solomon, Efrén and Apá readied the twins for bed. Unlike the last couple of nights, Efrén remained full of energy. He couldn't wait to hear all about the plan to bring Amá back.

But something about the way Apá slouched at the kitchen table scared Efrén.

He approached Apá and took a seat beside him. "What's wrong? Aren't you excited about getting Amá back?"

"Just a bit nervous. That's all."

"What do you mean? You raised the money, right?"

"It's not just about the money. Things are different than they were a few years ago. It's so much tougher now. So many people involved. Before we can plan anything, I have to get the money to your mother."

"How are you going to do that?"

Apá stared off into nothingness. "Without her ID, I can't wire money to her. So I'm going down to San Diego tomorrow. There's a fence near a state park. I'm going to try and sneak the money to her."

Efrén flopped back onto his chair. "Wait. But la migra's gonna be there. ICE could take you too."

"Mijo, sometimes the best place to hide is in plain sight. I'll blend in. Act like I have nothing to fear."

"No, you can't!"

"Shhh. Mijo, you'll wake up the twins."

Efrén nodded.

"Look, I know it's risky. But I don't have a choice. Even my friends who have permission to be here are afraid." He reached into his back pocket and pulled out a folded sheet of paper. "Here."

Efrén started unfolding it. "What is it?"

"My cousin's information. His name is Miguel, and he lives in Arizona. If anything happens to me, I want you to call him. He and I had a long, long talk today. He's a good guy and will come get you and the twins."

A rush of panic surged through Efrén's body. "Apá . . ." he said, pleadingly. "There has to be another way."

"No, mijo. There isn't. Only a born citizen is safe right now."

*Citizen?* Efrén's mind raced. "Apá, *I'm* a citizen."

Apá wasn't having it. "No. Ni siquiera lo pienses. The border is no place for someone your age."

"Maybe. But it's no place for Amá either. Or you. Please, Apá. I can do this."

Apá didn't answer. He simply pressed his hands together and sighed into them.

"Please, Apá," Efrén repeated. "I can do it."

Apá wouldn't meet his eyes.

"Look, I've taken care of Max and Mía. I've taken

them to school. Bathed them. Fed them, just like you needed me to. Please, Apá. Let me do this. For Amá."

Apá rubbed the back of his neck.

Efrén scooted forward. "You've always taken care of this family. You drag yourself to work when you've been sick, or even hurt. You and Amá have given me everything I need. Let me help. This is my family too."

Apá nodded to himself, then finally reached over and cupped his hand over Efrén's. "If we do this, we do it together. Is that clear?"

"Yes, Apá. Together. You and me, juntos."

"Okay. I will call your Amá. Set everything up. Mijo"—Apá swallowed hard—"I am very proud of you. You are very brave."

*Brave.* It was the exact opposite of how he felt.

# TWELVE

It was so early that the twins should have still been asleep, but the idea of buttermilk pancakes from Denny's had them both wide awake. They bounced in place while Apá reached into his wallet for one-dollar bills so they could play the claw machine—something they almost never got to do. Max pointed to a tiny panda bear with shifty button eyes while Mía ogled what could have been a koala or a badly sewn sloth.

"¿Quieres tratar?" Apá asked, extending a bit of playing money to Efrén too.

Efrén wasn't interested. It wasn't that he didn't like playing the game; it was that Apá was acting like this would be the last time he'd ever see any of them. Like he knew something he wasn't telling.

After topping off the twins with plenty of dessert,

Apá dropped them off with Adela, the tiny lunch lady whose duplex apartment doubled as the school's unofficial day care. She wasn't cheap, but she was kind and easygoing, and always wore a smile. All the kids loved being around her.

But even her smile vanished—turned all awkward and uneasy—when Apá handed her his cousin Miguel's contact information. Just in case.

With the twins taken care of, Apá made one final stop at the ARCO station to fill up the Chevy for the two-hour drive down to San Diego. Efrén sank into the passenger seat and waited inside the truck, feeling his stomach tighten as the numbers on the gas pump gauge rose. Even with its huge gas tank, the truck didn't seem to take long to fill.

Apá got behind the wheel and looked over at Efrén, as if giving him one last chance to change his mind. "¿Listo?"

"Yep. Ready." Efrén forced a smile. In spite of what Apá had told him over and over again—he really *did not* have a choice. Going into Tijuana alone was something he had to do. For Amá. For the entire family.

This was the only plan they had. He needed to be brave.

For the next hour or so, Efrén rested his head against the passenger window, catching the occasional sight of the blue waters of the Pacific. His eyes followed the white silhouettes of ships out on the ocean as well as the foamy trail that followed them like tiny snails. Efrén marveled at the thought that there were people out there—possibly entire families—enjoying the beautiful day. He tried imagining the size of the boats, wondering what it might feel like to have an ocean breeze hitting his face.

The slowing of traffic caught Efrén's attention. "Apá, is that a toll?"

"No, mijo. That's the San Clemente checkpoint. Don't worry. It's closed right now. The Border Patrol opens it randomly to catch people coming up from the border."

"But . . ."—Efrén shifted uncomfortably—"what if it opens as we come back?"

Apá patted Efrén's shoulder. "We slow down and let them wave us through. We'll be fine. Promise."

Efrén's stomach churned, but all he could do was lean on the door and let his face rest against the sun-warmed window that reminded him of hot chocolate, fresh estrellita soup, and the piojito scalp massages from Amá. Efrén could almost feel himself cuddling by her side, feeling her gentle fingers running through his hair, along with her firm but soothing nails sweeping along his scalp.

"We are getting close, mijo."

Efrén shut his eyes but stayed awake. He was nervous about crossing the border alone. Scared about what could happen. But thinking about Amá gave him the courage he needed.

*I've got to do this, Amá. For you.*

"This is it," Apá said, pointing to the large sign. "San Ysidro. Last US exit."

Efrén sat up as Apá turned off the highway and made a right over the bridge. Efrén watched the streams of people strolling along the sidewalk, most carrying backpacks—their ages as different as the shades of their skin.

Up ahead, a red trolley caught his eye. "Look, Apá. It's like a toy from one of those Thomas the Tank Engine table sets at the stores."

Only Apá didn't answer. He had other things on his mind. "Mijo, you have the money, right?"

Efrén patted the small satchel stashed secretly underneath his shirt. "Yep."

"What about the pesos for the taxi? Remember, you want to fit in."

Efrén searched his front pocket. "Check."

"And—"

"AND my identification card. AAANND your notarized letter of permission too." Efrén held up both items.

Apá pulled into a small parking lot. "I'm sorry, mijo. It's not you I don't trust."

"Don't worry. I know the plan. Go through the revolving doors. Follow the crowd until I get to the other side. Take a taxi down to Avenida Revolución . . . ask for the aro."

"Arco," Apá corrected, simultaneously miming an arch with his hands. "Like the station where we gassed up today. It's huge. You can't miss it."

Efrén knocked at his temples, as if forcing the information into his head. "Arco. Arco. Got it. Amá will be waiting next to it at the Taco Loco."

Apá nodded before stepping out of the truck and leading Efrén to a ramp heading toward the Mexican entrance. "Hasta aquí llego. I can't get any closer."

Efrén nodded, knowing that Apá had gone as far as he could. "I got this, Apá."

"Of course you do. Just remember: Act like you belong. And don't worry, I will be here when you get back."

Efrén walked up to a long concrete corridor decorated by curved metal blades overhead. He blessed himself, took a deep breath, and followed closely behind a middle-aged couple with three young boys, pretending to be their fourth. He went through the revolving doors, and before he could really figure out what had happened, he found himself at the other side, just like that.

Efrén searched his pockets, clenched the taxi money in a tight fist, and made his way down the cement walkway full of street vendors—a few as young as Max and Mía.

No matter how much it hurt him to see, Efrén knew he couldn't get distracted with other people's problems. He needed to stay focused. *Amá is waiting.* Thinking of her helped him quicken his step.

"¡Taxi! ¡El más barato!" a man called to him.

Efrén looked up. He was heading toward a row of

taxi drivers—all in street clothes—each vying for his business.

*Great.* All his life, he'd been told to never get into a car with a stranger. Now, not only was he doing exactly that, he was doing so in a foreign world he didn't know. Efrén surveyed the men, pausing at the oldest gentleman with the receding hairline. He was just about to approach him when the man took a puff from his cigarette.

*No, thanks.* Efrén hated the ashy smell.

Suddenly, a voice cried out. "Yo, little man. You need a lift?"

While the voice itself wasn't familiar, the way the man spoke was. It reminded Efrén of Rafa, back in the neighborhood. He turned to the man, still keeping a safe distance.

He wore distressed baggy blue jeans and a beige T-shirt that showed off his thick arms. He had a detailed tattoo of a baby girl that curled around his neck and a weathered face that somehow reminded Efrén of Apá.

"You speak English really well," Efrén told the guy.

"Yeah. After twenty-eight years in the US, I'd better." He looked around a bit. "Little man, you alone?"

173

Not sure of what he should say, Efrén stayed quiet.

"Man, this ain't no place for a kid like you. Name's Eduardo—people call me Lalo. Come on, I'll take you wherever you need to go."

Efrén hesitated at first but knew he didn't have much choice. "Can you take me to the Arco on Revolución Avenue?"

Lalo went all bug-eyed. "Downtown? You serious?"

"It's all right. I can handle myself."

"Nah, man," Lalo said. "I ain't dropping off a kid there."

"You have to." Efrén didn't see any choice but to admit, "I'm meeting my Amá there. She got deported."

The guy gave Efrén a quick look over. "Ouch"—he nodded—"that changes things. All right, little man. You got it."

Efrén followed him to his car and got into the back seat. Only there was no seat belt to be found, and it made him a little uncomfortable.

"So," Efrén said nervously, "you said you lived in the US. What are you doing here?"

Lalo laughed out loud, really loud. "It's not by choice, that's for sure. I got myself deported. That's pretty much all there is to it."

**174**

Efrén looked around at the stains and tears on the upholstery. "Why don't you find a coyote to get you back across?"

Again, he laughed. "Little man, you don't just go back. It ain't that easy."

Efrén studied the side of Lalo's neck tattoo. "Is your daughter here with you?" Efrén could see the man crinkle his forehead through the rearview mirror.

"Little man, you sure ask a lot of questions. And how you know I have me a little girl?"

"Your tattoo," Efrén said, pointing.

Lalo laughed. "Look, little man, I do what I can for her. She knows I love her. If I didn't, I'd have my lady bring her over here. So I could be with her."

"What do you mean?"

"It's simple. I love my girl. Want what's best for her. Look around. Do you really think *this* is a place to raise her? Nah, she's way better off in the US. There, she can make something of herself—be someone. Not like her old man."

Efrén went quiet and thought about what he'd said. "I don't get what makes Tijuana so bad."

Lalo finally offered a genuine smile. "This place is limbo, man. A place not quite Mexico, not quite the

US. La Tierra de los Olvidados—the Land of the For-gotten. You don't get a name like that for nothing."

Efrén tried to distract himself by reading every bill-board he passed. Beer. Clubs. Women. That's mostly all he saw advertised. But he simply couldn't get what Lalo had said out of his head. What if he was right? What if crossing over wasn't really an option? *If Lalo couldn't find a way to be with his own little girl, then what chance did—*

Suddenly, the entire city felt even larger than before. The cars. The people. They were all moving so fast.

Efrén couldn't let himself finish the thought. "Lalo. I gotta pee."

Lalo cut across the busy lane and pulled beside a zapatería and farmacia. "All right, little man," he said, pointing up ahead. "You gonna cross Benito Juárez Street and make a right. There's a McDonald's right there. Use the restroom, and then go across the market-place. You'll find the Arco de la Revolución up ahead. You'll be safe as long as you stay on this street. Be careful—ponte trucha. Do *not* go anywhere else and *don't talk to no police.* They can be dangerous too. Got it?"

Efrén nodded. "I got it." He stepped out of the car

and reached for the money. "How much I owe you?"

Lalo scoffed. "No way, homes. You go find your mom. That's all the payment I need, all right?"

"All right, Lalo. Will do."

And just like that, Lalo pulled away in what was probably an illegal U-turn. Efrén walked past an empty shoe polish stand and smiled as he set eyes on the two golden arches overlooking the entire street. *McDonald's?*

Suddenly, this place didn't feel as scary anymore. Maybe Apá was wrong. Maybe it wasn't as bad as he'd thought. Efrén patted his shirt, feeling for the hidden satchel underneath. And maybe, finding Amá was going to be a lot easier than he'd thought too.

# THiRTEEN

Peeking out from behind the McDonald's was the white Tijuana arch with a wide-screen TV entangled in the center, like a fly on a spiderweb, playing commercials. *¡EL ARCO!* This is the one he'd been looking for. Efrén thought it looked like the top half of a Ferris wheel—the kind the church sets up in their parking lot once a year—only this one didn't have any baskets to ride on.

*Finally.* He was so close to Amá he could feel it.

Everywhere he turned, stores—with their front shutters rolled up—were opening for business. However, even with all the zooming cars and street vendors hollering their best offers, the place felt strangely calm, as if the entire block had prepared for a huge block party and all the guests decided not to show up.

Efrén sidestepped a gray-haired man dressed in a complete mariachi getup, his eyes wide and friendly, his face full of years. The move caused Efrén to bump into the teenager attending to the newspaper stand. The teen, wearing faded jeans and a red tee, snapped harshly at him. "¡Cuidado!"

"Oh, disculpe," Efrén said apologetically.

He couldn't look like a tourist; he needed to act like he lived there. But blending in was going to be harder than he thought, especially with all the new and interesting things to see. All around him, vendors held up heavy fleece blankets—perfect for cold winter nights—colorful mesh bags used for grocery shopping, lucha libre wrestling masks, a variety of superhero piñatas, and the always popular Mexican sarapes.

What they were selling made perfect sense. What didn't was why they were all calling out to him in English. It was true that he was an outsider who didn't really belong—but how did *they* know this? Was it something in the way he dressed? The way he walked? Maybe the way he looked at everything with new eyes. He searched the crowd, comparing the sea of brown skin. The range was huge, an entire color swatch of different shades.

There were so many vendors there, people like Lalo, struggling to find their place in this strange world.

Just as a sadness began to grow in the pit of his stomach, a pair of kids, a boy and a girl, cut him off. In their hands was a pair of tin flowers made from stripped slits of Coca-Cola cans.

"Did you guys make these?"

Unsure of his question, the little boy and girl turned toward each other and shrugged. "¿Ustedes lo—?" But Efrén stopped himself mid-sentence as he looked down at their hands. There was no need to ask in Spanish. The answer was as obvious as the dirty Band-Aids at the ends of their fingers. Efrén remembered the pesos Apá had given him. But the number of pesos he had on him wouldn't be enough to help these kids. Efrén reached into his shirt and pulled out the satchel with the money meant for saving Amá.

From the wad of money, he peeled away a pair of twenty-dollar bills and handed them to the kids. It was the right thing to do. Efrén knew Amá would have done the exact same thing if she were there now.

But that didn't make what he'd done any safer. Efrén immediately tucked the satchel back under his shirt and looked around for any wandering eyes that might have seen him. Sure enough, he spotted two women staring at him, whispering something to each other.

What had he done?

Before giving either kid a chance to thank him, Efrén hurried through the marketplace as quickly as he could. But with each step he took, a little voice at the back of his mind warned him.

As Efrén made his way out of the marketplace, he thought about how lucky he was to have been raised on the other side of the border. He remembered all the times he'd secretly wished he were one of the rich kids that lived in the Floral Park neighborhood around his school, the times he wished he might have his own room, own TV, own bed.

None of those things mattered to him anymore. All he wanted was his family at home, in their tiny studio apartment, together.

Amá and Apá didn't like to talk too much about why they left their homes so long ago. "For a better life," seemed to be their only answer. Only now, Efrén was beginning to understand what they'd left behind.

Just as Efrén hurried past the last stand, something caught his eye. A few feet away stood the ruins of an aqueduct, the arch barely standing. It was the same

Roman like architecture he'd read about in his social studies books.

*Wait*. Which of the two arches was he supposed to follow?

He looked over at the giant silver landmark above, but the street under it appeared to end.

The aqueduct arch led to a colorful street, where he could see a hotel sign up ahead.

*That has to be the one*. The Taco Loco had to be nearby.

Efrén followed the aqueduct arches down the most colorful street he'd ever seen. It was as if each building had somehow been painted in a different fruit flavor. To his left and toward the bottom of a giant lemon-colored wall stood the opening to a tiny shop. Efrén skipped over many of the words on the homemade sign, finding comfort in familiar ones like *dulces*, *jugos*, and *paletas*—all the delicious snacks he'd find for sale in Don Tapatío's food truck back home.

To his right stood Hotel Santa Cecilia, painted in the color of the watermelon agua fresca Amá occasionally made in the summertime. This thought made Efrén feel better about where Amá had landed. He pictured her in the marketplace, making friends with the vendors like she did around the neighborhood at home.

That all changed, however, once he passed the lime colored Río Verde bar. With every step Efrén took, the bright fruit flavor colors on each building grew darker, as if coated by a layer of dirt and ash. He paused, noticing the woman standing at the curb, watching him. His eyes moved to the men across the street watching too. He quickened his pace until he reached the end of the block.

There, he looked over his shoulder. The men were close behind him and coming closer. Apá's warning echoed in his mind and panic set in.

Back in his neighborhood, he knew exactly which fences to climb, which apartments to run to, and which alleyways to avoid. Here, the dangers were new. He'd heard stories of people being picked up off the streets and never heard from again. He'd also heard about drug cartels and corruption.

He scanned the street, catching a glimpse of a papaya-colored building. *The Taco Loco?* Hoping for exactly that, he broke into a full sprint. This time around, he didn't bother to apologize to anyone he bumped into along the way. And still, the people he slammed into acted as if witnessing a panic-stricken kid running through the streets was simply an everyday occurrence.

Stopping at an Alto sign, he coughed and heaved with his hands resting over his knees. The only other street available looked even worse than the one he found himself in. Again, he looked over his shoulder. The men chasing him stopped as well, breaking into menacing smiles as if they knew something he did not.

"Hey, little man!" a voice called out.

He felt a surge of relief when he saw the familiar taxi skid over to where he was.

"Get in!" shouted Lalo, reaching behind him to swing the back door open.

Efrén turned to look back at the men who had been following him. They weren't smiling anymore. He jumped into the car, bumping the back of his head as the car's acceleration flung his body across the back seat.

"Whoa, little man. What are you doing away from the plaza? This is definitely not the place for a kid like you."

"I was looking for the Loco Tacos . . . to see my mom."

"If you mean el Taco Loco, it's about half a block from the marketplace." He pointed in the other direction. "That way."

Efrén rubbed his temples before looking down at his watch. It was just ten past noon. "Can you take me there now? My mom's gotta be there waiting for me."

"Nah, man. No can do. Those guys are dangerous. In ways you can't imagine. We better hang low for a bit. Trust me. If your mom is waiting for you, she won't go anywhere."

"But—"

"Sorry. You'd be putting both our lives in danger, not to mention your mother's."

Efrén didn't like the sound of that. "Well, what do I do in the meantime?"

"You can join me for lunch. That okay with you?"

Efrén's mind raced. He knew better than to talk to strangers. But what choice did he have? Like it or not, Lalo was his best bet right now. Besides, there was something about Lalo that made Efrén trust him.

Tijuana was different than Efrén had imagined. He stared out the window, marveling at the scraps of sheet metal used to cover what in some cases appeared to be walls of cardboard. Those homes that were lucky enough to include plywood and cinder blocks looked to have been built on top of each other.

"Lalo, why are the homes in the hills so . . ."

"Ghetto?"

"Well, yeah."

"This is the land no one wants. On this side of the border, the rich folk here all live on flat land."

Efrén's eyes roamed. This place was nothing like home.

Lalo's place wasn't much different from the rest of the neighborhood. Just a tiny room barely large enough to fit one twin mattress, one rickety bookshelf, and a propane burner to cook.

"I know it ain't much, but I mostly just sleep here. Besides, the less money I spend here, the more I can send my little girl." Lalo turned and pointed at a photo resting over a milk crate beside his bed. His daughter was about the same age as Max and Mía, but she had light, wavy hair and hazel eyes.

"She's adorable."

"It's probably my favorite. Anyway, little man, make yourself at home."

"You mind if I use your restroom?"

"Again?"

"Yeah, my stomach acts up when I get nervous."

"Well, you good now, bro. It's just outside, to the

right. If the door's closed, don't go in. One of the neighbors may be using it."

Efrén went out through the back door. The outside area wasn't much better.

Over to the side was the outhouse. He stepped inside and slid shut the plank of wood that doubled as a door. He looked down at the bucket of water stored beside the toilet, vowing to never complain about having to wait his turn at home again.

He layered the seat in toilet paper. When he was done, he picked up the bucket (he'd learned about this trick from Apá once when the water to their apartment was shut off) and emptied it into the bowl. Somehow, the toilet flushed.

Efrén refilled the bucket and washed his hands with the nearby hose, then hurried back inside where Lalo had prepared a set of instant ramen soups.

"Bro, you like Maruchan?"

"Do you have any Tapatío?"

Lalo pointed to a bottle beside the bunny ear TV antenna. "Come on now. What kind of a homie doesn't have Tapatío in his crib?"

Efrén smiled and ate half-heartedly.

"Hey, little man. Don't worry. I gots you. How 'bout

we go down to el Muro 'til things cool down."

Efrén checked his watch. "My dad's kind of waiting for me across the border."

"I know you wanna get back, but waiting around here isn't gonna get you there any faster. Come on."

"All right," he said, slurping the last of the noodles.

Efrén followed Lalo back outside and waited for him to unlock the back door of the taxi.

"Whatcha doing?" Lalo asked, sticking his head out the driver seat. "We're bros now. You can sit up front from now on."

Efrén dashed across to the passenger side and slid back into his seat, cool like Lalo did. "So what's this Moro you're taking me to?" he asked.

Lalo laughed. "The *Muro* is the iron wall that separates us from the US side. It ends where the ocean waves begin to form."

"Beaches? I've never heard of any beaches in TJ."

Lalo pointed up ahead as he made a turn. "See there. That's the Pacific. Same water on both sides of the wall."

Efrén leaned forward for a better look. "Looks kind of like the beaches at home."

"Yup." Lalo brushed the tip of his nose. "Sometimes

I come around here, buy myself a drink, and stare out into the ocean, thinking about my little girl. There's usually a parent or two running around with their kids. I gotta admit"—his voice broke a tiny bit—"it still hurts. Makes me feel robbed."

Efrén glanced over at him. "I'm sorry."

He scoffed. "At least I've got my memories to keep me company. Memories of me rocking her in my arms back and forth, of me making up baby rap songs about us." Lalo's jaw tightened. "You know what I miss most," he continued, while gazing out at the sea. "It's the way she used to look up at me . . . like she knew who I was. She didn't see a high school dropout, didn't see the tats on my arms or back. She just accepted me—unconditional love, bro. Anyway, my little Abby knew that I loved her and trusted that I would do anything and everything to protect her. Then she'd shut her eyes and be out for like three hours."

*Three hours?* It sounded like something Mía would do.

Lalo sniffed and exhaled deeply. "Yeah . . . three wonderful hours with her against my chest. Stuff like that has a way of changing people."

Lalo wiped the bridge of his nose.

Efrén wiped his eyes.

"The worst part is how the only memories she has of me now are behind the iron beams of the Muro. Lord knows I haven't lived a perfect life, but I ain't no criminal. Unfortunately, that's not how she sees me. To her, I'm nothing more than an embarrassment. Just some tatted up vato that sends her money and writes letters that she occasionally answers."

"She can write at her age?"

Lalo laughed heartily. "My baby girl isn't a baby anymore. That photo you saw is old. She's a teenager . . . with her own life to live. In the States, where she belongs."

Just like that, Lalo slipped a new CD into the stereo and cranked up the volume so loud that he cringed. "Check this out. It's my jam," he said, dropping the volume just a pinch.

Efrén had no idea who the rapper was, but he bobbed his head up and down as Lalo sang out loud. Efrén mumbled along as best he could, occasionally skipping over words he wasn't yet allowed to say.

Looking out the window was a glimpse of an entirely new world. Yes, the place was simple and poor looking, but it was also kind of beautiful. There were no ridiculous mansions hogging the ocean view or fancy hotels catering to the rich. Instead, there were tiny stands advertising fresh coconuts and shrimp cocktails.

"You know, Lalo, this place is kind of nice."

"It can be."

Lalo parked alongside a white curb that extended below a white lighthouse tower.

Efrén examined the miniature palm trees and uneven paths ahead. He couldn't decide if the place looked more like a skate park or miniature golf course.

"This is it. The Muro. Come on."

Efrén followed Lalo up the ramp, where families of every size lined the rusted iron beams, many in folding beach chairs. "What are they doing?"

"Visiting with families." Lalo pointed to the other side of the fence. "See, people from the US line up, and when their turn comes up, they get to hold hands with the family they're separated from. It's how I got to watch my daughter grow up."

Lalo placed his hand on Efrén's shoulder and paused like he had something to say. Only he didn't speak a word, just started walking toward the empty beach.

Efrén's eyes searched the many faces along the fence.

They came in all sorts. From babies to elderly folk with walkers—all different, beautiful shades of brown. Efrén began walking alongside the iron barrier. There were as many smiles as there were tears. A woman leaned into the space between the beams. She poked her arm through. She was about the same height as Amá, with a similar pinto bean shade of skin.

Efrén walked closer, curious about what she was doing. The answer hit him. Immediately, his eyes stung as if they'd been rubbed with a ripe jalapeño. Less than ten feet away was a mother and daughter—her Sea World hat still on—resting their foreheads against the other, each with their eyes closed, tears flowing.

He patted his shirt. Feeling the satchel underneath his shirt helped calm and reassure him. He looked over at the rest of the families camping around the sidewalk, waiting for their turn to hold hands too.

Efrén walked up to the iron fence and held up his palm against it. How was it possible that *he* was allowed to cross to either side? His place of birth didn't change anything about him. It didn't make him better than anyone else. It just made him . . . *lucky.*

Plain. Simple. Dumb luck.

Efrén came up behind Lalo and took a seat next to him, beside the invisible line where the ocean waves broke before retreating.

"Hey, you all right?" Lalo asked.

Efrén took a moment before answering. "I don't get it."

"What don't cha get?"

"Why people don't just hire a coyote and come over anyway. Like Amá's going to." His face lit up. "I know . . . you could tag along. You and Amá could cross together."

"Hold up," Lalo said, turning to face him. "It's not that simple. You can't just walk across."

"I know. That's why we got the money. My dad took on some extra night work to get it. But it's here with me. See?" Efrén reached under his shirt for the satchel and pulled out the wad of money he had. "Amá found a coyote who promised to get her across. Right at the hotel she found on the Avenida Revolución. All I need to do is deliver this to her. Then we can go back to the way things were. We can be a family again."

Lalo went silent.

"What's wrong? Is it not enough?"

"First, do us both a favor and put that money away." Lalo surveyed the beach to make sure no one was watching. "Look, man, as much as I'd like to, I'm not gonna lie to you. Getting across isn't as easy as you think. Using a coyote to cross along the customs line is pricey, but crossing over by the desert . . ."—he shook his head—"I wouldn't try it. Not again. And the local polleros are too risky. Some of them promise to get you across, but instead, they just take your money and dump you into the desert to fend for yourself."

"But they're not all bad, right?"

"Look, I know a few guys who work this area. I can't make you any promises, but I can call and see if they might be able to help you guys out."

"What about you? Don't you want to see your daughter?"

"Of course I do. More than anything else. But without a license or Social Security number, there isn't much I can do to make a living there. Besides, I've got a record . . . so if I get caught again, I'll definitely do some serious time behind bars." He rubbed his chin as he continued. "But you don't have to worry about me.

I'll make do. Sadly, it's what our people are best at—making do."

Efrén took a moment to let the words sink in. Then he looked at Lalo and tried reading the letters just below his knuckles, only the tattoo was too faded to read.

"Did you do something bad?"

"Nah, man. Well, nothing too serious." He stared out blankly at the sea as if entranced by the motion of the waves. "Simply put, I hung around the wrong type of friends . . . didn't think for myself."

Lalo gave Efrén a look. "Little man, do yourself a favor: surround yourself with good people. People who will bring out the good in you. Not the bad."

Efrén thought about David—about how lucky he was to have a friend like him. Scratch that. *Had* him as a friend. But it wasn't like he could just quit the election. Jennifer had been right. Él era una semilla, and he needed to push through the dirt and reach for the sunlight.

"I think you're a great guy. You shouldn't give up."

"Give up?" Lalo laughed. "Trust me. If there's one thing I don't do, it's give up. Here's the thing. All I want out of life is for my Abby to grow up happy, with a good job—maybe a family. That's it. Everything else is gravy." Lalo scratched at the tip of his nose. "I just want what every parent wants for their children: a better life."

Efrén's forehead wrinkled. "A better life? Without you?"

Lalo nodded ever so slightly. "A better life . . . for her."

# FOURTEEN

Efrén stared out of Lalo's car window noticing how everyone here was busy with work—even the kids. He craned his neck to follow a group of boys loading plastic crates into a tiny shop. In the US, these same kids would be busy skateboarding around town, or maybe burning off steam on the grass field of the neighborhood school.

*It's what our people do—we make do*. Lalo's words stuck around like the musky odor in the car.

"Here we are," Lalo said, parking the taxi outside a wax museum.

Efrén leaned over, catching sight of the giant Arco staring down at him. A nervous excitement now filled him.

"Come on," said Lalo, "your mom must be worried

mad about you." He pointed ahead. "Don't worry, I'll catch up."

Efrén bolted out of the car, anxiously scanning the area around him. And when that didn't work, he turned to Lalo who calmly jutted his chin at a rompope-colored Taco Loco restaurant. "Over there."

Without a blink, Efrén broke off into a sprint and didn't stop until he stood below the Club Super sign. Of course. This made perfect sense to him. Where else would Amá go? She was Soperwoman.

Amused and equally excited, Efrén rushed inside the restaurant where a lady behind a mosaic counter flattened out rolls of masa into perfectly shaped tortillas, like Amá used to do back home.

"Hola, buenos dias. ¿Algo de tomar?" the lady offered with a warm smile.

"No, gracias," Efrén answered, searching the Coca-Cola themed tables for Amá. "Estoy buscando a alguien."

"Wait . . . are you Efrén?" she asked.

Efrén crinkled his forehead. "Yes. But how—?"

"Your mother told me all about you." Her accent was thick, but her English was easy enough to follow. "She went down to the Arco to look for you. Made me promise I'd let you know if you came by."

He scampered down the street as fast as his legs would carry him. He ran directly under the huge landmark, huffing and puffing.

"Efrén!"

Efrén turned, catching sight of Amá, who was already running in his direction.

"Amá!"

Before he could say another word, Amá wrapped her arms around him and lifted him off the ground like she used to when he was younger.

Efrén closed his eyes and laughed as Amá began kissing every spot on his face.

Amá held on for one last squeeze before letting go of Efrén. Her glance shifted over to Lalo who now stood by, hands in pocket, smiling.

Efrén pointed at him. "Amá, this is my friend, Lalo. He helped me get here."

She sandwiched Lalo's hand between hers. "Thank you. I was so worried that something had happened to him."

"Not this kid. He's got real smarts about him."

Amá smiled and pointed toward the restaurant. "Would you like to join us?"

Efrén nodded at Lalo, who agreed. Amá and Efrén sat together on the same side of the table. "Guadalupe," she called. "¿Podrías tomar nuestra orden, por favor?"

The lady put down the masa and wiped her hands on her apron before coming over with a bowl of chips and salsa.

Lalo dug into the salsa with the warm tortilla chips, raving about the entire menu. He swore Amá had found one of the best places in all of TJ. Then he asked her where she was staying and how she liked the city.

Amá looked even more tired than usual, but continued to smile, even as she went over the details of her deportation. By the time Guadalupe brought in the tray of tacos covered in green sauce alongside grilled nopales and green onions, the topic had changed to coyotes and the dangers of trying to cross the border.

"I got ditched twice myself," Lalo said, squeezing lime on each of his tacos. "Then I dropped four G's on some fake papers but ended up getting arrested and sent back. Things are different now. Even if my daughter's old enough to petition on my behalf, they'll never give me permission. Not with my record."

He just stared at his food as if embarrassed to look Amá in the eye.

There was an awkward moment and all Efrén could do was swirl the straw in his Jarritos soda.

"But there are others who can get me across the line, right?" Amá asked, her words almost pleading.

"Yes," Lalo answered. "That kind of stuff's done by organized groups. But it's very expensive."

Efrén reached under his shirt and handled Amá all the money. "Speaking of . . . here you go. It's almost thirteen hundred."

Lalo looked at Efrén, then back to Amá. "We're talking ten to fifteen thousand. With no guarantee."

Amá's eyes welled up, even as she held onto her smile. "So all we need now is nine to fourteen thousand more."

"Like I told Efrén, I know what it's like being separated from family. Don't worry, I'll help you. I've made some interesting connections over the years. I can set something up for you, but this kind of money,"—he shook his head—"it won't be through the customs line. Are you all right with that?

Amá nodded nervously.

"Okay. Let me see what I can set up for you."

"Yes, please," Efrén chimed in.

Lalo took one last massive bite and pulled out his phone before excusing himself.

Amá scooted her chair closer to Efrén and cupped her hands over his. "Oh, mijo . . . Tell me. How are the gemelos? Is Max behaving?"

Efrén smiled and nodded. "Si, Amá. Both are good. They ask about you, a lot."

She rested her palm over her heart. "And your Apá? I worry about him so much. He's exactly like you." She took her index finger and ran it down Efrén's nose. "Bien guapos, los dos."

Efrén blushed. "He's doing fine." As much as he wanted to, he didn't mention anything about Apá's having taken on extra work or his having hurt his hand, or even the fact that he hadn't slept much since she'd been taken away.

She stared long and hard at Efrén in the same Amá way she did whenever he brought home a perfect report card or lopsided paperweight that she had no use for—even though she didn't own a desk. "¿Y tú, mijo? How are *you* doing?"

Efrén shrugged. "Fine, I guess."

"I know all this has been incredibly rough on you," she said. "Having to watch over your brother and sister—especially your brother—is not easy. Trust me, I know. But like your Apá, you never complain. Some-how, you just do what needs to be done . . . whether it's fair to you or not."

Efrén blinked faster and tried breathing through his nose—anything to keep himself from tearing up. But when Amá reached for his hands and pulled them toward her and kissed them, he couldn't help it.

Amá and Efrén laughed as they each wiped away their tears.

"Look at us," she said, "a pair of chillones."

Lalo returned to the table, tucking his phone back into his pocket. "It's all set. Tomorrow morning. Four a.m.—sharp."

Amá gasped, sharing a nervous smile with Efrén.

Efrén leaped out of the plastic chair and hugged Lalo, who uncomfortably hugged him back. "It will be through the hills though," he said. "Is that okay?"

"Hills? That will be easy." She turned to Efrén and smiled. "Did I ever mention how I got into California in the first place?"

Efrén shook his head.

Amá chuckled to herself like she did whenever she told one of her stories about growing up in Mexico. "I came into the US on the back of a motorcycle in one-hundred-and-five-degree weather"—she gestured to her belly—"while seven months pregnant."

Efrén's eyes just about popped out. "With me?"

Amá's smile shifted to the side of her face, just like Efrén's did whenever he smiled. "Sí. En serio. I'm not kidding. The van that was supposed to bring me over-heated. We were pretty much stuck in the middle of the desert with no food or water."

"No way," Efrén said in total disbelief.

"Sí, mijo. You were a real macetón. Had a head like a watermelon. But it worked out. One of the lookouts, a guy on a motorcycle, ended up having to give me a ride." Amá laughed again. "Picture me on the back of a Harley-Davidson, sporting a huge barriga. It looked like I'd swallowed a beach ball."

Efrén shook his head. "I can't believe Apá agreed to that."

"He didn't know. But"—this time, Amá burst out laughing—"you should have seen his face when he saw me pull up to the drop-off spot. I know it sounds crazy, but what choice did I have?"

Efrén looked over at Lalo. "Will my mom be safe?"

"My friend promised he'd look after her. I trust him."

Amá held up her glass, her smile now a tad more comfortable. "To a safe return to America."

Both Lalo and Efrén reached for their sodas.

"And to Lalo," Amá added, ". . . our guardian angel."

# FiFTEEN

As promised, Lalo delivered Efrén safely to the San Ysidro Port of Entry, to the same spot where they first met. Efrén couldn't understand why Amá was so emotional. After all, he'd be seeing her at home the next day. "Ay, Amá," Efrén said, complaining as she once again kissed his entire face. "I gotta go. Apá must be worried. I should've been back hours ago."

Finally, Efrén pulled away. "Te veo mañana. Okay, Amá?"

Amá wiped away her tears and nodded—but not before blessing him and delivering another round of kisses.

Efrén turned to Lalo and extended his hand. But Lalo wasn't having it. Lalo leaned forward and gave him a huge hug.

"What is it with you two and hugs?" said Efrén.

Everyone laughed, even Efrén.

Wearing a sad smile, Lalo held out his tatted-up arm and waved. Efrén thought about how he'd almost passed him up because of the way he looked. *If I hadn't met Lalo and those men had caught up to me . . .* Efrén couldn't let his mind go there.

He'd been lucky—very lucky—to have met someone like Lalo. How Efrén wished there was something he could do to help his new friend, to give him the second chance he so deserved. But for now, Efrén needed to get back to Apá, as well as Max and Mía, to help prepare for Amá's return home.

He waved good-bye to Lalo, sweeping his arm from side to side as widely as he could. Then he stepped into the concrete corridor leading back to the US. He looked up at the cameras glaring down at him and then at the guard carrying the largest military style rifle he'd ever seen.

So many images flooded past him: brown-skinned families reaching within the gaps of a US-built fence, forced to wear their best smiles; tiny kids like Max and Mía working day jobs to help their families make ends meet; elderly men and women selling handmade items, curbside.

A strange mix of sadness and pride overtook him, and for the first time in his entire life, he finally felt connected to his Mexican side. Everywhere he'd been, Efrén had witnessed signs of courage, people no different from himself refusing to give up. He shook his head, remembering all the times he'd corrected Max and Mía for speaking Spanish, insisting that they learn the only language that mattered. Now, he understood why Amá and Apá continued to speak Spanish to them, even when they themselves needed every opportunity to practice their English. He'd been born Mexican American. Only he'd forgotten about the Mexican part.

*Nunca olvidaré.* He would not forget. Efrén joined the end of a long line and waited in silence. He looked down at his ID, birth certificate, and notarized letter of permission—hoping they would be enough to get him back home. When his turn came, Efrén nervously handed his paperwork to the mustachioed officer.

"Reason for visiting?" the man said in a slight Mexican accent.

Efrén understood the Latino man was simply doing his job, but that didn't stop him from judging his choice of job. "To visit my mother," he said, looking up and giving the man a hostile look. "She got deported."

The officer put the documents down and paused, as if to find just the right words. "Go ahead," he said while handing everything back to Efrén.

Efrén reached over, but the officer gripped the forms and wouldn't let go. "These forms," he said, leaning forward and whispering, "represent a giant sacrifice from your parents. A true gift. Don't let it go to waste. ¿Entiendes?"

The words caught Efrén off guard, but he understood exactly what the man meant. "Yes. Completely."

And with that, the officer released his hold. "Next!"

Efrén hurried until he was completely outside the building. Just like that, he was back in the US. He paused for a second and looked around, wondering if he'd someday return to this land of broken dreams. The immigration officer had been right. He'd been given a real gift. One that allowed for him to return to Apá.

Efrén studied the flow of people and followed them until he saw the red trolley up ahead. Across from there, he spotted an antsy Apá pacing up and down the sidewalk in his black sweatshirt.

Apá looked up and sighed in relief, then turned around and got in his truck.

Efrén jogged over and jumped into the passenger

side. Before he could say a word, Apá reached across and hugged him closely like Amá had just done. "Mijo, I was so worried. What took you so long?"

"I got a little lost," Efrén said, still wrapped in Apá's arms. "But I found Amá and gave her the money. And guess what . . . she's gonna be crossing tomorrow morning. With the best coyote in town."

Apá unwrapped his son. "¿En serio? Tomorrow?" His lips rolled into a smile. He turned and tousled Efrén's hair. "You did good, mijo. I am so proud of you."

Efrén smiled back.

"And to think how close I came to running across and looking for you. I swear . . . if it wasn't for Max and Mía, I would have tried."

"Yeah," said Efrén, "I believe you."


With the long drive ahead of them, Efrén took the time to answer all of Apá's questions. Of course, there were lots of details that Efrén decided to leave out. As far as Apá needed to know, the trip had been a walk in the park.

While it hurt to lie to Apá, Efrén didn't see the point

in upsetting him. Hearing that Amá would be back soon had Apá happy and full of life. Efrén sank back in his seat, as Apá blasted the radio and sang along. For Efrén, it was like getting a tiny peek at what Apá must have been like when he was younger. Amá would always tell stories about outrageous things he did when they first met. How he'd run away from his parents' ranch for weeks at a time, showing up in nearby cities, looking for jobs that made use of his brains, not his hands.

"Can I ask you a question?" Efrén asked, his eyes still gazing out the passenger window.

"Sí, claro," answered Apá while bobbing his head to the music.

"Why did you and Amá leave Mexico in the first place? You and Amá seem to have so many great memories from there."

He lowered the radio. "It's a long story, mijo."

"That's okay," said Efrén. "It's a long ride home."

Apá laughed, this time turning off the radio completely. "Well, I'd just become a lieutenant in Mexico City . . . youngest one ever at the time."

Efrén could feel the pride in Apá's words.

"But then, the drug cartels began to get more and more power. Soon the government itself became corrupt—bien chuecos—and many of my own men began taking bribes for small favors. But those favors grew bigger each time. Then one day, some men from a maldito cartel stopped by. They wanted help releasing a few of their men. They gave me a choice. Help them out and get paid nicely or . . ."

Efrén's eyes widened. "What did you do?"

"I said no and tried holding my ground. But then . . . I got word you were on your way. I couldn't risk your or your Amá's safety. I got my temporary visa—"

"And Amá came over on the back of a motorcycle!"

Apá laughed hard. "She told you that story?"

Efrén nodded.

"Yes, mijo . . . we have lots of good memories there." He turned to Efrén. "But we've made new memories here. Three of them actually: you, Max, and Mía. And we wouldn't—"

Suddenly, his face turned pale.

Efrén looked up and suddenly saw a wall of red brake lights ahead of their car. Apá put on the brakes and then shifted in his seat, angling his head to get a better look ahead as traffic came to a crawl.

Efrén did the same. "What if the checkpoint is open? What if—"

Apá rested his hand on Efrén's shoulder, immediately easing his tension. "Tranquilo, mijo. Be calm. We will get through. Promise." He reached into his shirt pocket and pulled out two sticks of gum. "Here."

Efrén took a stick of gum with a blank look on his face.

"It's hard to look nervous when you're chewing gum. Trust me. It's an old trick I picked up a long time ago while on the force."

Efrén felt like he might need the entire pack. Nevertheless, he popped the gum into his mouth and began to chew.

"Just lean your head against the window and look really bored." But that was easier said than done.

Apá continued to crane his neck for a better look. "I can't tell if it's open or not. Too many big trucks."

Efrén pressed his forehead against the passenger window and crossed himself before shutting his eyes for a quick prayer. *Please, God, . . . let it be closed. Let it be closed.*

He suddenly felt Apá's hand tapping him on the shoulder. "Look." He pointed up ahead and cheered with the same kind of excitement he had when his Club América team scored a goal. "They're closed, mijo! They're closed!"

Efrén opened his eyes and caught Apá sighing deeply before sinking back in his seat with a smile. "See . . . told you we'd be fine."

Efrén let out a breath he didn't realize he'd been holding in. Again, he shut his eyes. Again, he blessed himself—this time thanking God for everything He'd given him:

*Thank you, Dios. For everything.*

*For Amá. For You keeping her safe.*

*For Apá, who never gives up on his family.*

*For Max and for Mía . . . who love me and make me feel like I matter.*

*For being able to live in the US.*

*For being able to go to school and not having to work instead.*

*For—*

The sudden acceleration of the car broke his thoughts. Efrén's stomach churned as they drove passed the unmanned station. The taste of the gum was now gone and this time, he spoke his thanks aloud: "Gracias, Diosito."

He looked back as the car sped up, his mind racing about what could have happened. Apá had told Efrén not to worry. That the border patrol officers would have simply waved Apá through along with the rest of the traffic. Why then, had Apá looked so worried?

# SIXTEEN

Efrén was glad to reach home, even if it was so late. All Efrén wanted was to get some rest. But first, they needed to stop by Adela's apartment across the street and pick up the twins.

Apá tried to pay her, but she wouldn't have it, saying all she wanted was for Amá to make it back soon.

Max and Mía had fallen asleep on the couch while watching *SpongeBob* reruns. Apá bent down and scooped up Max, while Efrén leaned in and picked up Mía.

Even with her light frame, she began to weigh on Efrén's arms by the time they made it across the street. Apá reached down and took her over his shoulder as well. Determined to help, Efrén rushed up the stairway and held the door open for Apá, who now strained with the weight of a twin on each shoulder. Max looked up and winked at Efrén, who followed closely behind. Efrén broke out laughing and winked back at Max.

Once inside, Apá lowered the little ones onto the mattress with the same care Amá always did. Even kissed the same spots on their foreheads. To think, sometime tomorrow, the coyote Lalo found would be returning Amá home, where she belonged. Efrén could almost feel her kisses pressing against his head again.

Too exhausted to undress, he kicked his shoes off and tucked himself between his brother and sister. "Good night, Apá," Efrén said mid-yawn.

"Buenas noches," he said, as he turned out the light.

Efrén shifted over, trying to avoid the annoying ray of moonlight that somehow always managed to seep in through the cracked window blind. Even with little light, he could see Apá lying down onto the mattress beside him, pulling up the covers, and blessing himself.

A thought raced through Efrén's mind. "Apá?"

"Yes, mijo?"

"You think we could go to mass tomorrow? With you?"

Apá laughed to himself. "Funny, I was just thinking the same thing. It's the least we can do to give thanks.

Now get some rest. You earned it."

Minutes later, just as Efrén's mind began to doze off, he felt a chubby foot poking the side of his face. But after everything he'd just experienced, he didn't mind anymore.

The next morning, a noise in the kitchen woke Efrén. He lifted his head and wiped his eyes.

*¿Amá?* For a split second, he thought she'd somehow returned. But his mind immediately set him straight; it was just Apá, standing over the kitchen sink.

Sunday mornings were usually the only day of the week when Apá got to sleep in while the rest of the familia attended eight o'clock mass. It wasn't due to a lack of faith though. No, Apá was very religious. He was just tired—a lack of sleep from the long hours he worked. But not today.

Efrén gently lifted Max's leg off him and headed to the kitchen. "Apá, ¿qué estás haciendo?" he whispered.

"Estoy limpiando."

Efrén paused to think. Apá was right. The place was a mess. There was no way he could have her come home to this. Not after all she'd been through.

He might not have been able to form steaming sopes with his bare hands, but he was able to clean a kitchen with the same speed and precision as Amá.

"It'll go faster if I help," Efrén said.

Apá shot him a smile before tossing him a cleaning rag.

Cleaning up such a tiny kitchen didn't take long— not with Max and Mía asleep instead of running around trying to help.

Efrén put the last plate in the cabinet as the phone rang.

Not waiting for a second ring, Apá just about flew to the phone. "Sí, ¿bueno?"

The moment was at hand. Efrén leaned in closer, trying to listen. "Is it her?"

Apá nodded, still listening attentively. The words coming over the phone were muffled, but the excitement behind them was clear as day. Efrén crossed himself and rested his head on his pressed hands.

Suddenly, Apá's entire face lit up and Efrén knew the news was good.

"¡Ya cruzó!" He put the phone aside and shouted. "She crossed! She's in San Diego. On her way home!"

A sense of joy surged throughout every inch of Efrén's body. He ran up to Max and Mía. "Wake up. Amá's coming home. Today!"

Never before had Max gotten out of bed so quickly. "Amá?" Tears flowed down his round cheeks as he jumped up and bear-hugged Efrén, who in turn picked him up and squeezed him before spinning him around.

"Are you sure?" Mía's soft voice asked.

Efrén lowered his little brother and knelt beside her. "Sí, Mía. I promise. This time it's for real."

A smile—a very special smile—now filled her face.

"Amá's coming home!" This time, it was Apá shouting at the top of his lungs. "She's coming home!"

And with that, Max catapulted himself onto the mattress and did the most spectacular flip anyone had ever seen him do. Apá and Efrén looked at each other and shared a nod. Before long, the entire family was jumping on the mattresses—including Apá.

Max and Mía paraded around the room in their freshly-ironed Sunday best. Apá stood back, looking bothered.

Efrén glanced at the crooked creases down Max's pant legs. "They're not so bad. It's not like you burned them."

Mía spun and swirled the lace skirt of her dress. "I think my dress looks beautiful."

"Yes, it does, mija," said Apá. "Bien bonito . . . but a bit short. You better put some shorts on underneath."

Apá turned to Max's snug-fitting pants. "Ay, mira no más. My little muffin boy." He tried squeezing a finger into the waistband. But when that didn't work, he simply rubbed his chin, thinking.

Efrén took a closer look. "Amá usually moves the button or sews in more fabric."

*More milagros.*

"Well, how 'bout this?" He went into the kitchen and pulled out the Velcro kit Amá sometimes used to hold up picture frames. He undid Max's front button and secured the Velcro along the front. "There. No one will ever know," he said, giving Max a gentle pat on the rear.

Efrén pointed to the clock on the microwave. "Apá, we'd better hurry."

"Apá checked his watch. Okay, mijos . . . why don't the two of you go brush your teeth and do your hair while Efrén and I stack the mattresses and make this place look nice for your Amá. And Max"—he turned right to him—"just a little Moco de Gorila gel in your hair."

Max smiled and shook his head hard as if it were a rattle.

Apá looked on with a crumpled forehead as the pair raced into the bathroom.

Efrén knew that look well. "What's wrong?"

"Nothing."

"Apá?" He tilted his head and gave him a look.

"It's just . . ." Apá sighed. "You guys deserve so much more than this. Pobrecitos—their clothes barely fit. And you. I'm sorry, mijo."

Efrén looked down at his own yellowing polo shirt and patched-up, navy blue pants. "Sorry for what?" he asked.

Apá glared down at the mattresses on the floor. "For all of this," he said, gesturing around to the entire apartment. "For failing you and your hermanitos. You guys shouldn't be living this way. A kid like you should have his own room." His eyes panned down to the mattresses on the floor before giving the nearest one a good, hard kick. "Or at the very least, an actual bed."

"Apá—beds are overrated. I don't need a bunch of fancy stuff to be happy. I've got my family. Well, by tonight I will. And that's more than a lot of people have. Trust me."

"You are an amazing kid. You know that, right?"

Efrén grinned from ear to ear. "I just try to copy you and Amá."

Mass felt a bit more special than usual. Before it even started, Apá knelt down, locked his hands tightly, and shut his eyes. Without missing a beat, Max and Mía kneeled alongside Efrén, no doubt praying for the same thing.

At the end of mass, Father Octavo announced the pancake fund-raiser happening in the courtyard. Once there, Apá pulled out a few dollar bills from his wallet and counted to himself. It was all he had left after donating the rest during mass. Apá ordered two meals, making a total of six pancakes, four strips of bacon, four sausages, and a pile of scrambled eggs to share.

After watching Max gobble up everyone's leftovers, the family walked back home. All Efrén could think of was getting ready for Amá's return. There was so much to do. First was picking the best roses from the apartment building's flower bed. Efrén, Max, and Mía each picked different colored roses; Efrén stuck to pink, while Mía and Max went for any shade they could reach.

They stopped by the fruit trees for a few treats to take home and made a quick stop at the 99 Cents Store. Using a pocket full of laundry quarters, Efrén bought two "welcome home" balloons for Amá, which of course, both Max and Mía wanted to carry back to the apartment.

The balloons drew the attention of the entire neighborhood. Everyone they passed stopped to ask if Amá was coming back.

"¿En serio?"

"¡Ay, qué bueno!"

The cries of support were everywhere. Soon, every woman Efrén had ever seen at the laundromat stopped by the apartment with a welcoming dish in hand: Fried taquitos, tostadas, elotes, mole, enchiladas, flan, carrot cake—you name it, it was there.

Efrén couldn't believe how many people they'd actually managed to cram into the apartment. It seemed everyone wanted to be there when Amá came back. But as the time passed, the worry started.

"No se preocupen de nada. Ese tráfico es maldito," said Don Ricardo with a smudge of guacamole at the edge of his mustache. And he was right. The I-5 was horrible. Amá was probably just stuck in traffic.

But soon, one o'clock gave way to two o'clock, and when the food had gone cold, people began running out of excuses. Especially Efrén.

By four o'clock, the apartment had emptied of all the guests. Efrén couldn't handle the thought of any bad news and avoided looking in Apá's direction, choosing instead to stare at the mostly untouched food that covered Amá's entire kitchen counter.

Finally, the phone rang. Apá rushed over to answer, followed closely by Max and Mía.

Efrén studied Apá's face for any sign of good news.

But what he saw instead was his father's face fall, his shoulders sink, and his eyes close. The news was bad. Very bad.

# SEVENTEEN

Apá didn't say much after hanging up the phone. He simply stood in place; his breath sounded like there was a terrible weight on his chest. With tears in his eyes, he finally coughed to clear his throat.

Efrén braced himself for the news.

Only Apá didn't say a thing. He couldn't.

There were so many thoughts, so many feelings scurrying around in Efrén's head—some so horrible that he couldn't bear the silence any longer. "Is she okay?" he finally asked.

Apá leaned in closer to Efrén—away from Max and Mía. "She's safe," he said, his voice thick and buried. "But the van she was in got pulled over at the San Clemente checkpoint. She's being held at a detention center."

Efrén was about to ask a question when he felt a tug by his pants pocket. It was Max looking up at him, big penny eyes gleaming with hope. "Is Amá almost here?"

Mía rushed to his side to hear the answer.

Efrén's throat swelled and choked him in a way he had never felt before. His mind flashed backward and forward all at once. He thought about Lalo watching his daughter grow up from behind a fence and imagined Max and Mía trying to squeeze their little arms through the fence just to hold hands with Amá again.

Efrén darted his teary eyes in the opposite direction and sucked in a breath. He wanted to be strong, wanted to pull himself together—for Max, for Mía. But he couldn't find the strength.

That's when Apá went down on one knee, first gently resting one hand on Max's shoulder, then another on Mía's. "Mijos, your Amá loves you two"—he interrupted himself and turned briefly to Efrén—"you three. And she will do everything she can to come home to you. And I will do everything I can to get her here. We will never give up. Nunca. That much I can promise you. But, no . . . she will not be coming home tonight. She will not be coming home tomorrow. Honestly"—his voice broke mid-sentence—"she won't be coming home anytime soon."

After sitting at the kitchen table in silence, Apá finally picked up the carrot cake and carried it over to the mattresses. "I don't know about you guys, but I am going to sit here, watch some cartoons, and eat this cake. Anyone want to join me?"

Efrén turned to Max who then turned to Mía who sat silently, still wearing her heavy frown.

Apá held up his hand and wiggled his fingers. "How about some piojitos?"

Max's head perked up. Piojitos were his favorite, but Efrén wasn't sure he'd accept them from Apá. After all, that was Amá's specialty.

Still, Max gave in. He picked up his fork and took a seat beside Apá, who immediately began scratching Max's head in little Amá circles.

"Mía?" Efrén held up his hands and waved *his* fingers at her. "They've been trained by the best," he singsonged.

Mía looked over at Max, who was now lying across Apá's lap with a mouthful of cake. "Okay. But don't expect me to like it."

It didn't take long—just three episodes of *Sponge-bob*—for the twins to eventually fall asleep. Apá took a towel to wipe away the smudges of frosting he could find on the blankets.

He and Efrén headed to the kitchen, where most of the food remained untouched.

"Such a waste, huh, Apá?"

Apá didn't hear. His mind seemed to be on something much more pressing. "Mijo, I don't have a right to ask this of you—it's supposed to be my job—but could you continue taking the twins to school and picking them up?"

Efrén lowered his head. "Apá? We are going to try again, right? Maybe with a different coyote? I can start collecting water bottles and taking them to the recycling center. Maybe I can—"

"Mijo," Apá interrupted, his eyes as red as Efrén had ever seen them. "Your Amá is being detained. I don't know what's going to happen."

Efrén was shaken to the core. "So that's it? We don't try again?"

Apá reached over and gently guided Efrén's chin up. "Look at me, mijo. I swear, I will not give up on your mother. That is a promise. ¿Entiendes?"

Efrén's emotions finally let loose. "And what are we supposed to do without her?"

"We make do. That's all we can do."

*We make do.* Lalo's words. Only now, they made less sense. "What if I don't want to make do? What if I want to be selfish? Apá, I'm not asking for a huge house with a pool or fancy toys. I'm just asking for Amá back. That's all. Why"—he asked between hiccupy sobs—"why can't I have that?"

Apá wrapped his arm around him. "I know, mijo. It's not fair. I know."

# EIGHTEEN

Once again, the sun's morning light squished through the cracked window blinds, hitting Efrén in the face. And once again, Efrén turned to see an empty mattress next to his. He got up and headed to the kitchen counter where the food, which hadn't fit inside the refrigerator, still sat. Most of the delivered items were made from recipes Amá shared with the women at the laundromat, so in a way, having the food was like having a piece of her here too.

Efrén's mind wandered back to when he'd said goodbye to Amá.

Amá was emotional; she kept squeezing and holding onto his hand. Efrén didn't understand. He assumed he'd be seeing her again the next day.

If only he'd known, he would have let her squeeze

him as long and as hard as she wanted. He wouldn't have minded her smothering him with endless kisses all over his face. In fact, he would have wrapped his arms around her and never let go.

But now, he had work to do.

Getting the twins ready went okay. He didn't say much. Neither did they. It wasn't until they arrived at school and saw Ms. Solomon in the playground yard that they finally cracked.

Without warning, Max raced to her side and gave her the biggest of hugs.

Ms. Solomon turned and bent down to greet him. But when Max wouldn't let go, her smile softened and she turned to Efrén, who was still carrying Mía on his back.

"Wow, I'm not sure I deserve *this* much love," she joked.

Efrén lowered Mía, but she grabbed onto his leg and wouldn't let go. "Look, Mía, your favorite swing is empty. Hurry, before someone beats you to it."

Only Mía wouldn't budge.

"Efrén, is everything okay?" Ms. Solomon asked.

Efrén took a moment to gather himself before finally looking up at her. He didn't have the strength to keep the secret bottled up inside anymore. "There was no job. My mom . . . Amá"—his eyes darted back to the ground—"she got deported and arrested for trying to get back home. We don't know if she'll ever come back."

Ms. Solomon gasped. "Oh, my God." She knelt down and gave Max the biggest of hugs. Mía let go of Efrén and joined in.

Efrén looked on, wishing he were younger, wishing he too could—

But before he could finish the thought, Ms. Solomon rose and draped her arms around him in the same way Amá would have done had she'd been able to in person.

Ms. Solomon took the twins into her classroom and promised to keep a close eye on them all day. Now Efrén could just worry about himself.

Politics were behind Amá being taken away, and so he wanted nothing more to do with them. The first step would be writing a resignation letter to Ms. Salas, letting her know that he was dropping out of the election.

The second step was simply getting through the school day without any more breakdowns. Avoiding David would be the first step.

Efrén arrived at school with plenty of time before

first period. Not wanting to run into David, he took a seat by the library staircase—the last place David would be found. Quickly, he penned his letter for Ms. Salas. He didn't go into detail, just stated he wasn't interested in running anymore. Then, he reached into his backpack and pulled out the copy of *The House on Mango Street*.

*Jennifer was right. This book* is *special.* Efrén knew exactly how the character Esperanza felt. She wanted to leave Mango Street behind as much as he now wanted to leave his tiny apartment on Highland Street. If he could, he'd change everything about his life. Especially that part about being the son of undocumented parents.

Efrén locked onto every word.

*"Like it or not you are Mango Street, and one day you'll come back too."*

*"Not me. Not until somebody makes it better."*

The lines grabbed at him, especially the somebody part. One thing was for sure, that somebody wasn't going to be him.

Fortunately for Efrén, the school bell rang just as he finished the last page. He got up and thought about returning the book but ended up tucking it back into his backpack to read all over again later.

He made a beeline for his first-period class. Sure enough, Mr. Garrett stood by the door, once again high-fiving students on their way in. Efrén gave him a forced smile. He could tell him what had happened later.

Efrén sank into his seat, making sure to angle his body in the opposite direction from David. He took out his agenda and stared at the calendar section. He couldn't think of anything worth jotting down.

He searched the pages for important dates. School elections, basketball tryouts, even the upcoming winter break—but they all meant nothing now. He closed his agenda and stared down at a black speck on the cover.

Suddenly, the door opened—Mr. Garrett had already started class. Someone was late. Efrén turned to sneak a peek.

His eyes went wide. *Jennifer?*

"Jennifer!" he called out.

The entire class all turned to look. Han ran over and gave Jennifer a huge hug.

"Ms. Huertas," Mr. Garrett called out. "Does this mean you will be joining us again?" His voice was hopeful.

Jennifer smiled widely and nodded.

Efrén watched as Han led Jennifer back to her old seat. He wanted to rush over and greet her, ask her how she managed to make it back. So when Mr. Garrett offered the chance to pair up with a partner for today's lesson, Efrén leaped out of his seat and hurdled over two rows of desks—all to reach Jennifer before Han.

This made Jennifer laugh. She turned to Han. "Do you mind?"

Han gave Efrén a look. "Go ahead."

Efrén took a seat next to Jennifer while Mr. Garrett added last-minute instructions on the board for a podcast assignment. "Okay," Efrén asked, "so how exactly did you get back?"

Jennifer leaned forward. "Ms. Salas. I emailed to tell her that I was dropping from the race. We ended up writing back and forth. She did some research, then called my mom. Told her all about the Fair Tomorrow Program that helps kids of color get into private boarding high schools all over the country. Ms. Salas is going to help me apply. Hey, maybe you should apply? Bet you'd get in."

Efrén shook his head. With Amá gone, there was no way he could bail on Max or Mía. "Nah. It's not for me." He glanced over to check that Mr. Garrett was still writing on the board. "Where are you staying?"

"Ms. Salas convinced my mom to let me stay with her until the program can find me a place. Technically, she's my foster parent."

"Wow. Ms. Salas really came through for you, huh?"

"Yeah she did. She's super nice, but I'm still getting used to living with her."

"So?" asked Efrén, "does this mean you'll still be running for president?"

Jennifer shook her head. "Can't. I have to focus on my application. Got to get ready for the entrance exam, practice for my interviews, *and* make up the work I missed. Besides, I saw your posters on the way over." She glanced over at David. "How's he taking it?"

Efrén lowered his head. "Not so good. We're not friends anymore. He made that perfectly clear."

Jennifer covered her mouth. "I'm so sorry. I never meant to pressure you."

"No. It's not your fault."

"Well," said Jennifer, "I'm glad you decided to run."

Efrén bit his lip. "I did. But now I've decided to quit. It's too much for me right now too." He padded his sweater pocket. "I just need to turn in my resignation."

"Oh," she said, sounding disappointed.

Mr. Garrett made his way to Jennifer. "Hey, Ms. Huertas. Just wanted to let you know that it's really nice having you back."

"Thank you. I'm glad to be back too."

"All right, but you two better get to work. You can catch up later."

"Yes, Mr. Garrett," the two answered at exactly the same time.

Later, when the end-of-class bell rang, Efrén saw a blur of yellow and blue—David's favorite colors—rush past him. Efrén let out a sigh as he waited for Jennifer and Han to gather their stuff.

The three left and headed down the main corridor together. "By the way," said Jennifer, "that poster by the drinking fountain is my favorite."

"Mine too," added Han.

Efrén blushed. "Oh, that's my little brother's. He meant well."

"Well," said Jennifer, "I think it's adorable." Jennifer rushed ahead to where Max placed the poster. Only when she got there, something was obviously wrong. She gasped and stood frozen as if she'd seen a ghost.

A kid stopped beside her. Then another. Each equally

wide-eyed. Efrén hurried over as kids began to huddle around. He couldn't believe his eyes.

## DEPORT
## EFRÉN NAVA ~~PRESIDENT~~ NON PRESIDENT
## "THE CHANGE YOU WANT TO SEE"

Jennifer shook her head. "I'm so sorry, Efrén. I can't imagine anyone doing something like this." Suddenly, Efrén heard someone calling for him. It was Abraham running toward him. Of course it was. Nothing ever happened at school without Abraham knowing about it.

"Ef-Efrén," Abraham struggled to catch his breath. "I guess el Periquito Blanco finally showed his true colors."

"What are you talking about?" Efrén asked.

"Our security guard, Rabbit, caught David messing with your posters. Took him to the main office."

Efrén didn't know what to say. He'd witnessed his apartment wall tagged up plenty of times before. He'd seen it being done as he peeked outside waiting for Amá to get home late at night. Even caught a few high school kids doing it on their way to school. But this was different. Way different.

This was David, making the horrible comments toward him. Toward his family. Toward Latino families everywhere. Even though their friendship was over, he never imagined that David could do something like this.

"No way," Efrén said. *Not him. This doesn't make sense.*

This was the same David who he'd shared so many bags of Cheetos with over the years.

The same David he'd gotten lost with on a school field trip to the LA Zoo, so that Apá had to drive over to get them.

This was the same David who loved to come over and sample Amá's delicious milagros—even the spicy ones.

"Whatcha gonna do about it?" asked Abraham. "You gonna beat him up?"

Efrén reached over, pulled down the poster, and crumbled it into a ball.

Jennifer tugged at his sleeve. "Han and I are going to check the rest of the posters. Why don't you go to the office?"

Efrén's chin fell to his chest. It was bad enough that the world didn't think that families like Efrén's were good enough for this country—but David too?

*Why, David? Why?* It was more than Efrén could take.

He handed the crumpled poster to Jennifer and walked away.

That walk to the main office was one of the longest of his life. *Deport Efrén Nava.* The words might have stuck to him like chewed-up bubble gum on the bottom of a sneaker, but they burned like the seeds of a hot pepper. He couldn't understand how David could be so cruel.

Efrén was about to go in when the door opened and David stepped out.

David gave Efrén a long, pained look.

Efrén opened his mouth, but again, the words failed him.

Mrs. Carey, the school principal, unexpectedly called out behind David, waving a yellow slip in the air. "I want you to take this note back to—Oh, Efrén . . ."

She panned over to David and then back at Efrén. The tension between them was obvious. "Efrén, why don't you come inside? There's something you ought to know."

David reached for the pass and disappeared up the stairs.

Efrén began to feel sick.

Mrs. Carey held the door open for him. "Come on in."

Efrén entered, the color drained from his face.

Mrs. Carey sat up. "School security caught David damaging posters. But he's not the person who wrote those racial epithets. In fact, he was going around the campus tearing them down. I can only imagine what you must have thought."

Efrén swallowed. "I thought that David was a horrible friend. A horrible person. And that I never wanted to see him again." His head tilted downward. "But it turns out I'm the horrible friend for thinking badly about him."

"Don't be so hard on yourself. A lot of us jumped to the same conclusion." She tapped on the desk with her pen. "Don't worry. We'll find whoever wrote those abhorrent comments. But first, you'll need to file a report. I will walk you through it."

Efrén felt terrible for thinking the worst of his best friend, or as David used to say, "his brother from another mother."

# NINETEEN

Mrs. Carey excused Efrén from the office a few minutes before the nutrition break bell. However, instead of lining up early and getting his lunch first, Efrén headed back upstairs to the quad area to wait for David.

When the bell rang, everyone passing by stopped and gathered, hoping to watch the biggest fight of the century.

Efrén didn't care about the kids circling him and asking questions. He looked around, finally noticing David coming his way.

But instead of shouting out insults at David like everyone around them expected, Efrén calmly walked over and extended his hand. The kids watching all booed and hissed before heading off in different directions.

"Thanks, David," Efrén said. "That was really cool of you. Even after what I did to you, you still had my back."

David just kind of shrugged. "Just returning the favor."

"Favor? What favor?"

"When I moved here, you never treated me differently, even if I was the only white kid on the entire block. You always called me an honorary Mexican and introduced me to your friends, and showed me the ropes. You even taught me all the Spanish words I needed—starting with the bad ones."

Efrén laughed. Suddenly, the world didn't feel like such a horrible place. Sure, there was someone on campus who didn't like Latinos, but right now, that didn't matter. Efrén had his best friend back.

"Well, I've got your back too," said Efrén. "That's why I'm dropping out of the race."

David shook his head. "No, thanks."

Efrén squished his eyebrows together. "Dude, you're my best friend. I can't run against you. You deserve it. You proved that today. Besides, after what happened to my poster . . . I don't want anything to do with any election."

David shook his head. "You can't quit. I was running just so people would stop thinking I was stupid. But I *would* be stupid if I let whoever messed up your posters win. No way. You will be"—he held up his hands in the air—"our next PRESIDENTE."

"I don't know. Besides, what about you?"

David smirked. "Vice president is more my style. Come on, F-mon, do it for your Amá."

Efrén looked up. "Wait. You know what happened to her?"

"Yep. My grandma heard about it while at the 99 Cents Store. Unlike you, she trusted me enough to tell me. Yesterday, I sat across the street from your apartment for hours, hoping to see your Amá again."

Efrén pressed his lips together—felt them trembling.

"F-mon," David continued, "why didn't you tell me?"

Efrén looked down at the ground. "I tried. It just hurt too much to say aloud."

David's eyes blinked overtime. "Dude." And without saying another word, he leaned forward and gave his F-mon the longest bro hug the school had ever seen.

"You forget. Your Amá's treated me like I was her son. More than my own mom, even. I'll never forget the year your Amá bought me a belt for my birthday. Said that she was tired of seeing my calzones."

Efrén started to laugh-cry. So did David.

"Seriously, this school needs you," said David, wiping his eyes.

"You really think I could make a difference?"

David nodded. "Yeah, I do. You taught me that the color of my skin doesn't matter. Only now, this school—heck, the whole world, needs to be reminded."

A voice chimed in. "Is this a private party, or can we join in?"

It was Jennifer, along with Han.

Efrén wiped his eyes dry. "We were just talking."

"Yeah, obviously," said Han.

Jennifer pulled Efrén's resignation letter from his sweater pocket and waved it in the air. "So, what are we going to do about what happened?"

"Yeah, Mr. Presidente?" added David.

Efrén reached for the letter and held it up close as if he could hear it speaking to him. He took a long breath.

"So?" asked Han.

Only Efrén didn't answer. He looked up ahead at the wrought-iron fence surrounding the school and sighed.

He walked up to the cold fence, curling his fingers

around the solid bars. He thought back to el Muro, the border wall. Back to the faces he'd seen. Men, women, and children waiting in line to see the people they love.

*Muro kids*. That's what he, Max, and Mía were now. From now on they'd each have to poke their fingers through the bars simply to feel Amá's touch.

Her touch. Something Apá would now be without. With him unable to go anywhere near the wall, he would never get to see her again.

*NO!* Efrén could not give up.

He would *not* give up on back scratches, morning sopes, or the funny character voices Amá made during bedtime readings. Ever since he could remember, he'd seen Amá and Apá pulling off different milagros out of thin air. Whether the miracles were scraping together money for food or sewing together a pair of pants out of one of the house towels for the twins to wear, Soperwoman and Soperman always found a way of providing for the family.

He would NOT be a Muro boy.

Not today. Not ever!

David, Jennifer, and Han came up to him.

Efrén turned to them. "I can start a campaign to educate parents. Let them understand their rights.

Maybe get a few schools to join us. You guys will help me, right?" Efrén asked.

Everyone nodded.

"Okay." With his mind finally made up, he tore the resignation letter in half. There would be no quitting today. No, for all the semillitas like him, he couldn't stay buried any longer.

The time had come for him to be the change he wanted to see.

The time had come for him to be Soper too.

To be . . . *Soperboy.*

# GLOSSARY

**Adiós, mijos. ¡Los quiero mucho!** — *Bye, kids. I love you all so much!*

**Agua fresca** — fresh flavored water (usually made with fruit, roots, or herbs)

**Ahora, ¿cómo consigo más dinero para cruzarla?** — *Now, how am I supposed get more money to get her across?*

**Amá** — term of endearment for Mom

**¡Ándale, burro!** — *Come on, donkey!* (Comparable to a horsey ride)

**Apá** — term of endearment for Dad

**Apá, ¿qué estás haciendo?** — *Dad, what are you doing?*

**Apestoso** — stinky

**Aquí están.** — *Here they are.*

**Arco** — arch

**Arco de la Revolución** — a giant arch (historic landmark in downtown Tijuana, Mexico)

**Arroz con leche** — rice and milk dish, similar to tapioca pudding (served for breakfast)

**Avenida Revolución** — Revolution Avenue (a major street leading to downtown Tijuana, Mexico)

**Ay** — Spanish interjection used to show frustration or pain

**Ay, Amá.** — *Oh, Mom.*

**Ay, amor . . .** — *Oh, love . . .*

**Ay, mira no más.** — *Oh, just look at you.*

**Ay, muchacho. ¿Qué tanto estás comiendo?** — *Oh, boy, how much are you eating?*

**¡Ay, qué bueno!** — *Oh, good!*

**Ay, qué cosa tan inútil.** — *Oh, such useless things.*

**Barriga** — belly

**Bien, Apá.** — *Good, dad.*

**Bien bonito** — very pretty

**Bien chuecos** — really crooked

**Bien guapos, los dos.** — *Very handsome, the two of you.*

**Bienvenidos, niños.** — *Welcome, children.*

**Buenas noches.** — *Good night.*

**Buenos días.** — *Good morning.*

**Cafecito** — coffee

**Cajeta** — similar to caramel, made with goat's milk

**Calzones** — underwear

**Chancla** — sandal or flip-flop

**Chet-tos** — common mispronunciation of Cheetos

**Chillones** — colloquial term for "crybabies"

**Chisme** — gossip

**Chismosos** — nosy, meddling people

**Churros** — fried dough treat(s) sprinkled with sugar and cinnamon

**Chusma** — riffraff, troublemakers

**Claro que sí.** — *Yes, of course.*

**Comadres** — relationship between a child's mother and godmother (also a term of friendship among close friends)

**¿Cómo están los gemelos?** — *How are the twins?*

**¿Cómo sigues?** — *How are you doing?*

**Concha** — bread roll with a crunchy, shell-like sweet topping

**Coyote** — nickname given to people who deal/arrange

transport of undocumented people across the US border

**¡Cuidado!** — *Careful!*

**Cundina** — a money pool where people contribute and take turns receiving a large share of money. Also called a "tanda"

**Dios(ito)** — God

**Disculpe.** — *Excuse me.*

**Don** — title of respect, similar to using "Mr."

**Doña** — title of respect, similar to using "Mrs."

**¿Dónde está Amá?"** — *Where is Mom?*

**Dulces** — candy

**Efrén . . . te amo. Muchísimo.** — *Efrén . . . I love you. Very much.*

**¡EL ARCO!** — *THE ARCH!*

**El Chapulín Colorado** — comic Mexican superhero (aka The Red Grasshopper/Captain Hopper)

**El Cucuy** — Latino version of the boogeyman

**Él era una semilla.** — *He was a seed.* (Metaphor)

**El Muro** — Mexico–United States border wall

**Elote(s)** — corn

**¿En serio?** — *Seriously?*

**Enchilada(s)** — a rolled tortilla lightly fried and covered in chili sauce

**Ensenada** — a coastal city near the border of Mexico in the Baja California Peninsula

**¿Entiendes?** — *Understand?*

**Eres una semilla.** — *You are a seed.*

**Estoy buscando a alguien.** — *I'm looking for someone.*

**Estoy limpiando.** — *I am cleaning.*

**Excelente** — *Excellent*

**Farmacia** — Pharmacy

**Flan** — a spongy, custard-like dessert sweetened with condensed milk and vanilla extract

**Frijoles** — beans

**Frijoles, frijoles, de las comidas más ricas, ¡lo más que comes, lo más que pitas!** —*Beans, beans, the magical fruit. The more you eat, the more you toot!*

**Gatito(s)** — kitten(s)

**Gemelos** — twins

**Gracias.** — *Thank you.*

**Gracias a Dios (Diosito).** — *Thank God.*

**Gracias, maestra.** — *Thank you, teacher.* (The title of "teacher" is used as term of respect)

**Guacamole** — an avocado dip containing tomato, onion, and lime juice

**Guayaba(s)** — tropical green fruit with a soft, sweet middle, aka guava

**Hasta aquí llego.** — *This is as far as I go.*

**Hermanitos** — siblings

**Hola, buenos dias. ¿Algo de tomar?** — *Hello, good morning. Something to drink?*

**ICE** — Immigration and Customs Enforcement

**Jarritos** — a popular brand of Mexican fruit-flavored soda sweetened using cane sugar

**Juez** — a judge

**Jugos** — Juices

**La migra** — slang for immigration enforcement, such as the US Immigration and Customs Enforcement (ICE)

**La migra la tiene. Los descarados de ICE la recojieron buscando trabajo en una fabrica.** — *Immigration enforcement has her. The despicable people at ICE picked her up while searching for a job.*

**La Sra. Solomon me dejó los niños. Están bien.** — *Ms. Solomon left the children with me. They are fine.*

**La Tierra de los Olvidados.** — *The land of the forgotten.*

**La Virgen María** — The Virgin Mary

**Lalo** — nickname for Eduardo

**¿Listo(s)?** — *Ready?*

**Lucha libre** — Mexican style of wrestling

**Macetón** — stubborn

**Maldito cartel** — deplorable cartel

**Mariachi** — traditional Mexican band

**Masa de maíz** — white maize flour used mostly for tortillas, sopes, and tamales

**Mentiroso** — liar

**Mi mamá no tiene papeles.** — *My mother is undocumented.*

**Mija** — term of endearment for a girl (or "my daughter")

**Mijo** — term of endearment for a boy (or "my son")

**Mijos** — my children

**Mijo, despierta.** — *Son, wake up.*

**Mijo, les hice un caldito de pollo bien rico. Por favor, entra.** — *Son, I made you guys a yummy chicken soup. Please, come in.*

**Milagro(s)** — miracle(s)

**Moco de Gorila** — a popular brand of hair gel in the Latino community

**Mole** — a popular Mexican sauce (similar to barbecue sauce) made with hot peppers and chocolate

**Muro kids** — a term used to describe children who only see their family across the border fence wall

**Nescafé** — a brand of instant coffee popular in Latino culture

**Niños** — kids

**No. Está bien. Déjala. Es demasiado pequeña para entender.** — *No. It's fine. Let her be. She's too young to understand.*

**No, gracias.** — *No, thank you.*

**No, gracias. Tal vez después de la escuela.** — *No, thank you. Perhaps after school.*

**¡No importa!** — *It doesn't matter!*

**No, le robaron su bolsa con todo su dinero. ¡TODO! Incluso el dinero que pedí prestado.** — *No, they took all of her money. EVERYTHING! Including all the money I borrowed.*

**No. Ni siquiera lo pienses.** — *No. Don't even think about it.*

**No. No sé. ¿Qué puedo hacer?** — *No. I don't know. What can I do?*

**No se preocupen de nada. Ese tráfico es maldito.** — *Don't worry about anything. Traffic can be awful.*

**No seas payaso.** — *Don't be a clown.*

**No te preocupes de nada.** — *Don't you worry about a thing.*

**No te preocupes, hijo. Tu madre volverá. Te lo juro.** — *Don't worry, son. Your mother will return. I promise.*

**Nopal(es)** — edible cactus plant

**Nos quisieron enterrar, pero no sabían que éramos**

**semillas.** — *They tried to bury us, but didn't realize that we were seeds.*

**Nunca** — never

**Nunca olvidaré.** — *I will never forget.*

**Oye, estoy muy orgulloso de ti.** — *Listen, I am very proud of you.*

**Paletas** — frozen fruit bars

**Pan dulce** — Mexican sweet bread

**Para presidente** — *for president*

**Pediche** — someone who repeatedly asks for things or lives off others (freeloader)

**Periquito Blanco** — "White Parakeet"

**Pesos** — Mexican currency/money

**Piojitos** — made-up term for scalp massage (literally "little lice")

**Pobrecitos** — poor kids

**¿Podrías tomar nuestra orden, por favor?** — *Could you take our order, please?*

**Polleros** — nickname given to people who physically transport undocumented people across the US border.

**Ponte trucha.** — *Stay alert.*

**¿Por qué no se van a ver la televisión?** — *Why don't you go watch some television?*

**Presidente** — president

**Pronto, mijo. Te lo juro.** — *Soon, son. I swear.*

**Pulparindo** — Mexican candy made with tamarind fruit, sugar, salt, and chili peppers

**Puro** — pure

**¿Qué puedo hacer?** — *What can I do?*

**¿Qué te pasó?** — *What happened to you?*

**¿Quieres tratar?** — *Want to try?*

**Ranchero** — ranch style cheese

**Rompope** — eggnog-like drink that usually contains rum

**San Ysidro** — border town on the US side

**Sarape(s)** — traditional blanket that usually has striped patterns and bold colors

**Semillitas** — seeds

**Señora Nava, ¿cómo está?** — *Ms. Nava, how are you?*

**Sí** — yes

**Sí, aquí está, escuchando.** — *Yes, he's here, listening.*

**Sí, ¿bueno?** — *Yes, hello?*

**Sí, claro.** — *Yes, sure.*

**Sí. En serio.** — *Yes. Seriously.*

**Sí, gracias.** — *Yes, thank you.*

**Sí, mijo. ¡Ay, cómo te extraño!** — *Yes, son. Oh, how I miss you!*

**Sí. Sí entiendo.** — *Yes. I understand.*

**Sí. Sí. Hablaremos más tarde.** — *Yes. Yes. We'll talk later.*

**Solo (solito)** — alone

**Somos semillitas** — *We are small seeds.*

**Soper** — Efrén's own personal take on the word super (combination of the words sope and super)

**Sopes** — fried round saucers of corn dough topped with refried beans, cheese, lettuce, and choice of meat (salsa is optional)

**Sus caras se les van a quedar así.** — *Your faces are going to freeze like that.*

**Taco Loco** — (literally "Crazy Taco") restaurant in Tijuana, Mexico

**Tajín** — a type of lime chile powder used on fruit and vegetables

**Takis** — a spicy brand of rolled, lime flavored corn tortilla chips

**Tamarindo** — tamarind

**Tapatío** — a brand of hot sauce

**Taquitos** — rolled and fried tortillas usually stuffed with meat, potato, or beans

**¡Taxi! ¡El más barato!** — *Taxi! Lowest price!*

**Te veo mañana.** — *I'll see you tomorrow.*

**Telenovela** — soap opera

**Tía** — aunt

**Tijuana** — a Mexican border city

**TJ** — abbreviation for Tijuana

**Tortilla** — a thin flatbread made of corn or wheat

**Tostada** — fried corn tortilla topped with refried beans, beef, lettuce, tomato, and salsa

**Traficantes** — (drug) traffickers

**Tranquilo** — (be) calm

**Travesuras** — mischief

**Traviesos** — troublemakers

**Troquita** — food truck

**¡Un gatito!** — *A kitten!*

**¿Ustedes lo—?** — *You guys—?*

**Veladora** — religious prayer candle

**¿Y Apá?** — *And dad?*

**¿Y tú, Mía? ¿Estás ahí?** — *And you, Mía? Are you there?*

**¿Y tú, mijo?** — *And you, son?*

**¡Ya cruzó!** — *She (Amá) crossed!*

**Zapatería** — shoe store

# ACKNOWLEDGMENTS

First and foremost, I need to thank my children for asking me to write this book. The request came at a time when I had pretty much given up on my dream of ever seeing my work published. Still, I wanted to write something special for them. Something that mattered. Something that highlighted the beauty of our Mexican lineage. Something that would help them to see that our people are worth being written about. Something to make them proud. They both provided me with the energy and motivation to make this happen.

I also need to thank my wife, Esther, for being there for me on the long nights, for picking up the slack whenever my energy gave way, and for her love and support. I could not have done this without her.

To write this book, I took parts of my own childhood

(both good and bad) and intertwined them with parts of my present life. Because of this, I thank everyone who ever played a positive role in my life. This includes my entire family: Abigail, Isaac, Esther, Francisco, Martha, Jeff, Alma, Edgar, Karla, Willie, Destinee, Marco, Max, Mía . . . and of course, my Amá, María Elena (the heart and soul of this story).

Thank you all for being *soper*.

This book exists because of you.

However, my thank-yous don't end there. None of this would be possible without my amazing and talented agent, Deborah Warren of East West Literary, for seeing my potential and believing in me even when no one else did—including myself. You have my eternal gratitude.

Special thanks to my editors, Rosemary Brosnan and Jessica MacLeish. I thank you both for helping to shape my book into the novel of my dreams. I cannot imagine having gotten through this experience without the two of you by my side.

To the entire HarperCollins family, especially the amazing copy editing team: Nicole Moreno, Rita Pérez, Gweneth Morton, Alexandra Rakaczki. I thank you all for making each and every page shine.

Thank you to Jay Bendt for coming up with such a brilliant book cover. It is everything I could have wished for—and more.

I'd also like to thank Denise Deegan and Susan L. Lipson for all of your invaluable feedback during the manuscript's earliest stages.

And where would I be without the most incredible critique group in the world, the Tightens. Jesper Widén, Beverly Plass, Alan Williams, Sonja Wilbert, and Heather Inch-Desuta . . . I thank you for taking me under your wings and for always being there for me.

A special shout-out to Mary Carey, Sandra Rubio, and Juana María Cordova Ornelas for all of your support and encouragement over the years—and for looking over all those bad, early drafts.

Lastly, I would like to take a moment to thank all of my students (both past and present) for their continuous support. It has been an honor teaching (and learning from) you throughout my career. There is a bit of each and every one of you in all that I write.